COUNTRY LEGACY

SHIPMENT 1

Courted by the Cowboy by Sasha Summers
A Valentine for the Cowboy by Rebecca Winters
The Maverick's Bridal Bargain by Christy Jeffries
A Baby for the Deputy by Cathy McDavid
Safe in the Lawman's Arms by Patricia Johns
The Rancher and the Baby by Marie Ferrarella

SHIPMENT 2

Cowboy Doctor by Rebecca Winters
Rodeo Rancher by Mary Sullivan
The Cowboy Takes a Wife by Trish Milburn
A Baby for the Sheriff by Mary Leo
The Kentucky Cowboy's Baby by Heidi Hormel
Her Cowboy Lawman by Pamela Britton

SHIPMENT 3

A Texas Soldier's Family by Cathy Gillen Thacker
A Baby on His Doorstep by Roz Denny Fox
The Rancher's Surprise Baby by Trish Milburn
A Cowboy to Call Daddy by Sasha Summers
Made for the Rancher by Rebecca Winters
The Rancher's Baby Proposal by Barbara White Daille
The Cowboy and the Baby by Marie Ferrarella

SHIPMENT 4

Her Stubborn Cowboy by Patricia Johns
Texas Lullaby by Tina Leonard
The Texan's Little Secret by Barbara White Daille
The Texan's Surprise Son by Cathy McDavid
It Happened One Wedding Night by Karen Rose Smith
The Cowboy's Convenient Bride by Donna Alward

COUNTRY
LEGACY

A COWBOY TO CALL DADDY

USA TODAY BESTSELLING AUTHOR

Sasha Summers

ISBN-13: 978-1-335-52329-7

A Cowboy to Call Daddy
First published in 2017. This edition published in 2022.
Copyright © 2017 by Sasha Best

For questions and comments about the quality of this book, please contact us at CustomerService@Harlequin.com.

Harlequin Enterprises ULC
22 Adelaide St. West, 41st Floor
Toronto, Ontario M5H 4E3, Canada
www.Harlequin.com

Printed in U.S.A.

Sasha Summers grew up surrounded by books. Her passions have always been storytelling, romance and travel—passions she's used to write more than twenty romance novels and novellas. Now a bestselling and award-winning author, Sasha continues to fall a little in love with each hero she writes. From easy-on-the-eyes cowboys, sexy alpha-male werewolves, to heroes of truly mythic proportions, she believes that everyone should have their happily-ever-after—in fiction and real life.

Sasha lives in the suburbs of the Texas Hill Country with her amazing family. She looks forward to hearing from fans and hopes you'll visit her online: on Facebook at sashasummersauthor, on Twitter, @sashawrites, or email her at sashasummersauthor@gmail.com.

To all the cowboy lovers out there!
You know a real hero when you see (read) one!

Chapter 1

After a leisurely drive admiring wildflower-laden fields, open pastures, and acres of cattle and horses, Eden's morning took a sharp U-turn back into Sucksville. Only this time she wasn't trapped at work, she was stuck in unknown territory. Boone Ranch Refuge was far off the beaten track, smack-dab in the middle of the Texas Hill Country. Things had been looking up when she turned off the two-lane county road and driven through the impressive wood and stone archway that assured her she'd reached Boone Ranch.

Her sudden flare of nerves wasn't surprising. She had a lot to do and a limited time to do it. And this time, she was determined to earn her father's respect. Did she wish there was another way? Yes, definitely. Her mother's support of Boone Ranch Refuge had been unwavering. And on paper, the work done here was worth funding. But her father insisted things weren't as on the up-and-up as they seemed. So Eden was here—without her father's blessing—to look deeper, review every scrap of paper, bill, invoice and ledger. Her father might believe that his word was enough to sway the board's opinion, but Eden knew better. Before she left, she'd make sure her father and the board were satisfied.

Logically, she needed to start at the refuge. But dropping in on a grantee for a surprise audit was a first. Normally, she'd give her applicants a checklist of what she needed and time to get everything in order. But this was different. She had a job to do and not much time to do it. The infamously prickly Dr. Boone would have to deal with the inconvenience. Still, she suspected he wouldn't be pleased. But dealing with Dr. Boone would be worth it if she left with information that made her father happy.

The sun poured into her small black rental car, so she kicked up the air-conditioning and drove on, bouncing over a cattle guard. The farther she drove, the more removed from the real world she felt. Ambling cows and a herd of red-and-white goats dotted the sprawling pastureland. It was peaceful and quiet, soothing to her frazzled nerves. She bounced across another cattle guard and dodged a wild-eyed roadrunner.

But her drive was cut short when the car's engine sputtered. She coasted to a stop, staring at the dash. No lights. No beeping. No clicks. And no air-conditioning. Just dead. She opened the door, the heat immediately stifling in the small car, and sat there hoping something miraculous would happen. Like the car starting. She closed her eyes, rested her head on the headrest and tried to think.

But when she opened her eyes, she screamed, pressing herself back into the car seat to avoid the massive black horse that had shoved its head inside the tiny car, putting them eye to eye. And scaring the crap out of her.

Her scream made the horse skitter back, knocking its head on the door frame, sliding on the red dirt and sending rocks flying in its wake.

She pried her fingers off the steering wheel and covered her face. What was wrong with her? It was a horse. A horse. On a *horse refuge*.

Her fingers sought out the three turquoise stones on her braided leather bracelet. Three stones, three words. *Take a breath.* Krista, her counselor, said it was a centering phrase. *Take a breath.* Sometimes—like now—Eden substituted her own words. *Keep it together.*

Yes, having an immobile car was inconvenient. And her dead cell phone, which she'd been charging in the car, was no help. But she wasn't the damsel-in-distress type. Was she thrilled about the two-plus-mile trek ahead of her? No. Not at all. She was irritated and hot, but none of this was earth-shattering.

That included an excessively inquisitive animal. She glanced out the door at the giant black horse. A horse that was already too close again, its thickly fringed eyes focused on her.

She met the animal's unwavering gaze. "Would you please back up?"

The horse didn't move.

She took a deep breath and slowly climbed out of the car.

The horse flicked its ears in her direction, the head rose, big brown eyes blinked. She stood, her back pressed against the hot metal of her car, and waited. But the horse didn't move, so she did. And scraped her ankle against the side of a cactus.

"Damn it." She pulled her leg back, stooping to examine the spot. Two sharp needles stuck out of her pale skin. Her sweat-slick fingers made pulling the thorns free a challenge. One she cursed through. By the time she was needle free, her skin stung. "*Damn* it."

The horse snorted, loudly.

"My skin's not as tough as yours," she muttered, glaring at the glossy black face. *You're talking to a horse.* Upside, it couldn't argue, yell or demean her. Best conversation of her day so far. "It's been a shit day," she added, because there was no one to reprimand her for her unladylike language. Even stranded and overheated, there was something freeing about not having someone looking over her shoulder, criticizing her every word and deed.

She'd barely finished her morning cup of tea when she'd had her first fight of the day with her father. He resented her reminder to take his meds and avoid stress. Next, a fight with her brother about what the word *deadline* meant—a suggested timeline, Greg's take, or an actual due date and cutoff, Eden's perspective. His frustration toward her over *his* misunderstanding never failed to amaze her. But Greg always found a way to make everything her fault. By the time she'd hurried home to hand the girls off to her ex-husband, Clark, she was ready to cry. Considering how distracted and impatient Clark had been, Eden's concern over her daughters' first multi-night visit with their father escalated. And the girls…

She swallowed. Thinking about her baby girls right now wasn't smart. They were with their father. For all his failings as a husband, he was trying to be a good father. But Eden knew the only reason she wasn't hyperventilating over the separation was because Clara, her wonder nanny, was with them. Eden didn't know how she'd ever survive without the older woman—not with the hours she kept and the stress she shouldered.

Stress. She could deal with stress. It was a constant in her life. Like now. Stuck here. Alone. With a black horse staring at her, invading her personal space—almost nose to nose.

"Is this some sort of horse greeting?" she asked, trying not to flinch as the horse sniffed her head and chest. *It's just a horse.* Granted, it was a huge black horse, but what's the worst it could do?

The horse made a strange sound, shaking its head and flipping its long, matted mane before clacking its teeth together.

What did that mean? Should she be worried?

No, she wasn't going to worry. If she ignored it, it would leave her alone. She hoped.

She shaded her eyes and peered down the dirt-and-rock road. Since she hadn't seen a car or truck in the last twenty minutes, she might as well start walking. She tugged her wheeled computer bag from the backseat and tucked her almost-empty water bottle into the side pocket. She had no other luggage. Because the last fight she'd had this morning was with the airline. For reasons unknown, they'd sent her suitcase to Arizona. But they'd happily offered to deliver it to the Lodge, the bed-and-breakfast housed on Boone Ranch where she'd be staying, as soon as it was located.

The cloudless blue sky was endless—no hint of any reprieve from the late-August afternoon heat. She twisted her hair, clipping it high on the back of her head, and set off down the red dirt road, dragging her wheeled briefcase behind her. She was not going to acknowledge the big black horse following directly behind her.

Take a breath.

Keep it together.

It was hot. Her black jacket, black pencil skirt and heels were soaking up the heat like a well-wrung sponge. She tugged off her blazer and tucked it over the strap of her wheeled briefcase. Her white camisole was much cooler. She could only hope her SPF 35 sunscreen would save her from getting too burned.

It was rugged country, with rock outcrops, twisted oaks, brightly colored wildflowers and needle-heavy cacti. But it was gorgeous in a wild, untamed way. The *chirp* of songbirds, the *whir* and *hiss* of the cicadas, and the rhythmic *clip-clop* of her traveling companion's hooves offered a complementary soundscape.

Her heel caught between two rocks, so she paused, tugging her shoe free. What she wouldn't give for her tennis shoes right about now. The horse, however, didn't stop. When she had her shoe back on and she was on two feet again, the horse...hugged her. His massive head rested on her shoulder, offering her what she could only consider an embrace—minus the arms.

She laughed; she couldn't help it. "You're a charmer, aren't you? Let's keep going."

The horse swished its tangled black tail, brown eyes fixed on her and ears perked up.

Eden set off again, stopping only when her shoes were too full of rocks or dirt to walk comfortably. And every time she stopped, so did the horse.

By the time she reached the refuge, she was overheated, dripping sweat and thoroughly exhausted. But even dehydration and throbbing feet didn't diminish the fact that Boone Ranch Refuge was impressive. Too bad her phone wasn't working; she could take a few pictures of the place her father was hell-bent on closing down. A place her mother had always championed.

Something large and solid bumped her between the shoulders, almost knocking her off her feet. She glanced back at the horse, tentatively rubbing her hand along its thick neck. "I'm assuming that's home." She kept her voice low, the same soothing tone she used when her daughters were sick or upset.

The horse snorted, pushing his nose into her chest.

"I'm going, I'm going." She smiled at the horse before hobbling forward, her briefcase bouncing along, rattling loudly.

When she walked under the arched Boone Ranch Refuge sign, she breathed a sigh of relief. First order of business, kicking off her shoes. The sooner, the better.

Several men formed a sea of cowboy hats. They stopped to stare at her as she headed toward the steps of the building with the small sign that read Refuge Office and Education Center. A building she hoped would house a bathroom. And ice-cold air-conditioning. And a comfy chair.

"You've got a shadow," one of the cowboys said, hurrying to take the handle of her bag. "Let me help." He smiled, pushing his hat back on his forehead.

"I've got it, thanks." She glanced back, the black horse still tracking her. "He's determined."

"He been following you for long?" the man asked, his megawatt smile a little too phony for her. Clark had a similar smile. She'd never fall for that again.

"My car broke down past the second cattle guard. He's been with me ever since."

"He pulled a Houdini this morning—doesn't

like being fenced in. Always seems to find his way home around dinnertime." He laughed, shaking his head. He *was* very handsome. "Count yourself lucky. Fester's been known to bite the hand that feeds him more than once."

She glanced at the horse, grateful Fester deemed her un-bite-able. Maybe the horse didn't like megawatt smiles, either. She fanned herself, hot, tired and out of patience. "I'm looking for Dr. Archer Boone?"

"Well, that's a shame. I'm his cousin, Toben Boone." His demeanor grew a little too friendly for her liking. So she leveled him with her most professional—and most icy— stare. His eyebrows kicked high on his forehead, but his smile didn't dim. "Fair warning. Fester might be on his best behavior, but my cousin's in one hell of a bad mood." He shrugged, calling out, "Archer, there's someone to see you."

She didn't miss the head-to-toe sweep Toben Boone gave her. Or the way it ratcheted up her irritation. *Please, God, don't let Archer Boone be anything like his cousin.*

The glass door opened slowly. A tall man with sandy blond hair stepped onto the porch, his attention riveted on the papers he held. This was *the* Dr. Archer Boone? With all the degrees, special certifications, awards and recommendations? He looked...like a cowboy. Jeans, plaid shirt, boots. Younger than she'd thought. Fit. And strikingly handsome.

His pale blue eyes barely looked her way, the slightly confused and disinterested expression a stark contrast to Toben's openly appreciative assessment.

She waited.

Archer looked up, his gaze narrowing. "There's Fester." He rested a hand on his hip, nodding at her horse companion. "Think you can put him in a pen that'll hold him this time?"

She didn't miss the "this time." Or the way Toben Boone's smile dimmed.

Archer looked at her again, as if only realizing there was someone else on the porch. His expression went from confused to openly hostile.

"You're late." Disapproval was clear in his voice. "Follow me." He disappeared inside without another word.

She stared after the man, in shock. Late for what? No one knew she was coming.

"That's Archer," Toben said. "I'd tell you he's a son of a bitch, but it's not right to talk about family like that." He winked at her. "Good luck."

Eden stood on the porch, still gripping her briefcase. Her feet hurt, her ankle throbbed, and she was exhausted. And now she had to deal with Dr. Archer Boone, who was, apparently, an ass. She stiffened her spine and followed him inside. He might not know it yet, but she held the fate of his refuge in her hands. And she could be just as cold and condescending as he was.

It took everything he had not to yell at the well-dressed young woman standing in his office doorway. But he wasn't going to hide his frustration. She was the reason for it. "I don't have a lot of time to get you situated." He brushed past her into the hallway, heading toward the makeshift office he'd prepared for her.

Was she wearing perfume? Did she think wearing a suit and nice perfume would make up for being three days late?

"Dr. Boone—"

"No apologies necessary." He headed down the hallway, opening the door next to his office. "Close quarters. This room is for storage but you should have everything you need to get the books in order." What was her name again? The temp agency had sent an email with all of her information. Amber… Amber Larkin?

Miss Larkin followed him into the office, pausing inside the door. Her face was expressionless, but he got the distinct impression she wasn't thrilled with her work space. What did she expect? Some fancy office? He didn't do fancy. If it wasn't practical, he had no use for it. The small folding table, beat-up desk chair, lamp and handful of multicolored pens he'd placed in the Boone Ranch Refuge mug should be all she'd need. He frowned, opening the blinds to let in some natural light.

From where he stood, he could see the chutes, walker wheel and paddocks surrounding the refuge office. This morning's arrivals, four horses so thin he could count their ribs, huddled together on the far side of the nearest pen. He needed to be out there, sorting them out and getting them settled. Not held up here with her.

"And the *books*?" Miss Larkin spoke up. "Where are the—"

"Right," he interrupted again, lifting the two paper boxes full of receipts, invoices and check stubs onto the table. "It's a mess." He patted the top of the box with his hand.

She looked at the boxes, then leveled her

unflinching gaze at him. "I can take it from here."

Her cool dismissal caught him off guard. For the first time, he looked at her. He sighed, seeing a distraction for his employees—and his cousin. She was pretty. Not flashy, overly made-up or attention-grabbing. Naturally pretty. Feminine. Soft. With long blond hair tumbling from the knot on the back of her head.

Damn it.

If he had time, he'd call the agency again and ask them to send someone else. But they'd stopped returning his calls. And he didn't have time to waste.

Her hazel eyes met his, unflinching. Almost irritated.

"Do you have any questions, Miss Larkin?"

"Miss Larkin?" she repeated.

He sighed. "You are Amber Larkin? Expected to be here three days ago? From Austin Clerical Temps? Or are you her replacement?"

She nodded, a slight crease forming between her brows.

"Apparently there's been some sort of mix-up." He'd never use Austin Clerical Temps again. "But if they've sent you, I'm sure you're qualified. I'm under a tight deadline, and as much as it pains me to admit it, I need help." He spoke quickly, rushing through the words. The faster he showed her around, the faster she'd get to work.

She hesitated, her eyes narrowing slightly before she asked, "Would you be so kind as to inform me of the particulars, Dr. Boone?"

He ran a hand over his face. "The short version? One of the refuge's largest benefactors sent me a review letter. We've never been under review before, so I suspect this is bad. Especially since Mr. Monroe isn't a fan of my work or my family." He broke off, shaking his head.

"You know him? Mr. Monroe?" she asked.

He shook his head. "No. His wife." He sighed. Chitchat could wait. "Without her support, I'm concerned we'll lose funding from the Monroe Foundation. But I'm not giving up." He glanced out the window, the sights and sounds of the only place he'd ever belonged easing some of the pressure on his chest. "You have one week to straighten out the financials my last bookkeeper neglected for who knows how long."

She stared at him for a long time. So long, Archer wondered if she was about to bolt.

"When did the bookkeeper leave?" she asked, her face revealing nothing.

"Nine months ago. The four temps I've been through weren't a good fit. I'm not easy to work with, I'll tell you now. And I don't like relying on strangers, but I don't have a choice. I know this is a job for you. But this is my life's work and I'm asking for your help." He leveled her with his most piercing gaze. "Are you able to do that?"

Her light hazel eyes never wavered from his, as if she was considering her options. The longer she remained silent, the more anxious he became.

She nodded, her eyes shifting from him to the boxes. "Eden." She didn't extend her hand. He didn't offer his. "Eden… Caraway."

"Archer Boone."

She didn't strike him as the temp type. If anything, she was more the uptight CEO type he forced himself to associate with at benefits and fund-raisers. She radiated money. Nice clothing. Perfume. She fiddled with a shiny turquoise-and-silver bracelet on her slim wrist. Everything about her was…elegant. But why would a wealthy woman take a temp job? On a nonprofit horse refuge?

He didn't care. At all.

Whatever her story, whatever her situation, it didn't matter.

The letter from Jason Monroe's office had been an unexpected shock. The last eighteen months, his entire family had succumbed to a frenzy of weddings and babies. He was the only brother left standing. No wife. No kids. No interest. His legacy was Boone Ranch Refuge. He was proud of his work and knew the next generation, nieces and nephews, would carry it on. As long as he had funding.

He frowned.

The Monroe Foundation was a big component of that funding. *That* was what mattered. Making sure he didn't lose their support. Books and receipts sat boxed and forgotten, needing to be sorted and cataloged, every cent accounted for. He didn't envy the job Miss Caraway was facing. But it was *her* job. As long as all the *i's* were dotted and *t's* were crossed, Miss Caraway could dress and look and smell however she wanted. Convincing Mr. Monroe and his board of trustees that the refuge needed funding was all he cared about.

"There's coffee in the cabinet in the break room. Pot's there." He nodded in the general vicinity of the small room, anxious to see to the new horses.

"I'm fine." She moved around the table, set her briefcase down and opened the paper box, peering inside.

"Need anything?" He hesitated, feeling the need to smooth things over. She hadn't run for the hills, always a good sign. He could stay on his best behavior—something that didn't come easily to him—if it kept her here until things were ready for Monroe. Yes, her being pretty was damn inconvenient, but there wasn't much he could do about that. He'd keep her busy here, poring over paperwork and away from roving eyes. She'd be here a week. Ten days tops.

She glanced at him, the slightest narrowing in her eyes unnerving. "My car broke down, inside the main entrance. Past the second cattle guard."

"You walked?" He glanced at her feet. Heels. She was in heels. And a slim-fitting skirt. Her white shirt was thin, the skin of her upper arms and chest pink from the sun. His gaze returned to her face. She'd walked all that way and she had yet to complain. And surprisingly, she knew what a cattle guard was. Maybe they'd get along fine.

"I walked. Your big black horse followed me." Her tone was clipped.

"Fester?" *Damn it*. The horse was more trouble than he was worth. "Did he bite you?"

She shook her head.

Which was a relief. But unusual. "Fester bites everyone." *Everyone*.

Her expression grew more rigid. "He didn't bite me."

He frowned. "That's good." That horse was a riddle Archer couldn't crack.

"You don't seem pleased." One brow rose.

He didn't appreciate her implication. He was relieved. The last thing he needed was a lawsuit over a horse bite. "I assure you, Miss Caraway, it is a relief." No lawsuit and no reason to further delay getting down to work. As far as he was concerned, she could make up for the lost days by working through the weekend. But they could talk about that this evening, *after* she'd put in a full day's worth of work. "I'll let you get to work."

She nodded, glancing out the window. She froze, her features coming to life. A deep crease formed between her finely arched brows, her full lips parting in a silent gasp.

He followed her gaze to the four horses in the pen outside. "We'll do the best we can to heal their bodies and their spirits. It never

fails to amaze me how resilient animals are."
It never failed to inspire him, either.

"What happened?" she asked.

"Drought conditions in West Texas are bad.
Drought meant no grass and dry water tanks."
He shook his head. "They're all that's left of a
wild herd. We wrangled 'em up and brought
'em here before it was too late. It's what we
do here, help out when no one else will."

Her wide hazel eyes focused on the horses.
His work could be ugly, revealing the cruelty
that existed in the world in a hard-to-take,
in-your-face way. Her expression shifted, revealing a mix of pain, sadness and despair.
It was a logical reaction. But he looked at the
horses and saw hope. They were here, alive,
safe, protected. He'd take care of them.

She was staring at him then. And something sparked in the depths of her eyes, something that held his attention. Her voice was
low, husky, as she said, "Where will they go?"

"We find them homes. There are just as
many folks willing to welcome them into
their families as there are those who treat
them badly or turn them out." He didn't mean
to stare back at her, but looking away was a
physical impossibility.

He didn't like it. He didn't like it at all.

He cleared his throat once, then again. "I'll check in later," he murmured, nodding in her general direction before heading outside. He turned, almost running into the door frame as he hurried from the office. He knew he had work to do, but right now, he needed to clear his head.

Heat slammed into him as he pushed through the front door. He stopped, resting his hands on the porch railing, and sucked in a deep breath. The song of the mockingbird, the whinny of the horses and the whisper of the hot wind slowly eased the off-kilter sensations agitating his stomach.

She was there for one reason and one reason only. He needed her to make him look good on paper. She was the accounting expert. He was the horse expert. And until she managed to get everything whipped into shape, until Mr. Monroe arrived and he'd acquired the extra funding, the only interesting thing about Miss Caraway was her work ethic. Because there was a lot of work to be done and not much time to do it.

Chapter 2

Eden flipped through her file on Dr. Archer Boone and the Boone Ranch Refuge. After four hours of sorting receipts—and making a slight dent—she deserved a rest. She was just as impressed as she'd been the first time she'd read his file. Renowned veterinarian and animal behaviorist. Studied internationally, devoted to environmentally friendly and ecologically minded practices. Graduated early. Went on to get several specialty certifications. But horses were his true gift. Clearly, the man was passionate about his work.

She respected that. And already well versed with his résumé, she expected that. She hadn't expected him to be so abrupt. Intense. Or condescending. Of course, he didn't know who she was—that would impact the way he treated her. Not yet.

The biggest surprise was how ruggedly attractive he was. Eden found him exceptionally handsome. More than once she'd found herself watching him out the window in the tiny makeshift office. He had a presence, one that made an impact. And watching him made a few things immediately clear.

Archer Boone did not like people. At all. Sitting in her lumpy office chair several hundred feet away she could hear the snap to his words and impatience in his voice when speaking to the men who worked there.

But everything about Dr. Archer Boone changed when he was working with his horses. He went from rigid and tense, impatient and frustrated, to fluid and graceful. She couldn't hear him, but there was no denying he spoke to the animals. Their ears pricked toward him, their gazes riveted. They seemed almost mesmerized by him. It was no wonder. He cared about them. Deeply. And the horses knew it.

"Are you the new bookkeeper?" A tall woman stood in the door. Jeans, worn brown boots, a sun-faded checkered blouse and a straw hat hung around her neck by a cord. "You don't look like you're ready to run. Yet." She had a nice smile. And vibrant blue eyes.

"Should I be?" She tried to look nonchalant as she pulled another file on top of the one she'd been reading. A temp would not have a file on her employer.

Eden glanced at her, but the other woman just shrugged.

"Sorting papers isn't the most exciting way to pass the time, but I have no complaints." Eden was cool, her heels were off, and she'd refilled her bottle with cold water and washed the dust and sweat from her hands, face and neck. Considering the way her day had started, sitting here sorting receipts in uninterrupted quiet was a welcome relief.

"The last four he brought out here did. I'm not sure it was the paperwork. Or if it was my darling brother and his...way with words." She pushed off the door frame and stuck out her hand. "I'm Renata Boone—the sister."

"Eden. Eden Caraway," she murmured, shaking Renata's hand. It wasn't a complete lie. Her married name had been Caraway—which she'd dropped as soon as the divorce was done. But after what Dr. Boone had said, she couldn't admit she was a Monroe.

Oddly, she had no knowledge of the review letter Archer Boone received. Odd, because she was the one who sent the review letters. Alarm bells were ringing. Why hadn't her father told her about it?

But the alarm bells weren't new. They'd started ringing when he'd been so eager to send her off on her "long-overdue vacation." Her father was a workaholic. He didn't do vacations, not in the traditional sense. Vacations always mixed business with pleasure, turning a Mediterranean cruise into the ultimate networking opportunity. That was why she was here, changing her reservations from the Palm Springs spa he'd booked to an extended stay in Stonewall Crossing. She would show him she was capable and indispensable and worthy of respect.

"The savior," Renata tacked on. "You might not know it, but you're important. Archer's freaking out over the dreaded Monroe visit, worrying they'll decide his request for funding will be denied—even though they've never denied him. I say he's being paranoid. He says it's a feeling."

Renata's blasé delivery was almost callous,

but Eden stayed quiet. Renata's words hit a little too close to home for her liking. Her father had all but said those very words. He'd made up his mind that the Boone Ranch Refuge no longer needed the funding, that it was time to give other worthy nonprofits a chance. And even though going against something her mother had been so passionate about was hard, Eden knew this was an opportunity she couldn't pass up. If she helped her father pull funding here, maybe he'd finally see her as the asset she was. *Please, God.* Getting out of bed already feeling like she'd failed was mentally exhausting.

The tension headache she thought was gone began to pulse slowly at the base of her skull.

"Don't get me wrong, I love my brother." Renata frowned. "And I support him one hundred percent. But I worry over how consumed he gets by this place sometimes. He holds on so tight. This review thing has turned him into high-stress, grumpier-than-ever Archer. Which makes for *miserable* family dinners."

She glanced out the window at Archer Boone. He was nose to nose with a skin-and-bones red horse. The horse was blowing into his hands, looking exhausted—defeated.

"Surely the refuge doesn't rely on the Monroes for all its funding?" Eden asked, need-ing to ease the guilt choking her. She knew the answer: the refuge received funding from a variety of places. The real question was: Why was Monroe funding so important? "It doesn't make sense for a nonprofit to rely on one source of support. Or for a foundation to agree to be a sole funding source, for that matter."

Renata perched on the edge of the beat-up table. "It's the whole tradition thing. Mrs. Monroe only visited twice, but she cared about this place, my father, my family and the people who live here. She'd talked about starting an endowment but then... Well, Mrs. Monroe's death was tragic and unexpected." Renata glanced out the window at her brother.

Eden was reeling. Her mother had vis-ited—been actively involved in—the refuge? She'd cared about this place, enough to form an endowment? She swallowed, still process-ing. "Is there a reason Monroe would pull funding?" she asked, hoping Renata might shed more insight.

Renata shrugged. "Not on paper, no. Ar-cher's work is hard to argue with. I have my suspicions, though."

Eden waited, wiping her palms on her skirt.

"Suspicions?" Why was she encouraging the woman? She should ignore her and pretend that the pile of invoices in front of her was riveting. But she waited, holding her breath, to hear what Renata Boone had to add.

Renata smiled. "Chalk it up to being the only girl in a house of men, but I think it's a personal thing. Am I assuming a lot here? Yes, yes I am. But my mother had hinted that things weren't good between Mr. and Mrs. Monroe, that Mr. Monroe and my father had a falling-out, that she'd stayed here to clear her head. Maybe now that his wife is gone, he wants to remove painful reminders?" She shook her head. "I could be way off. I've never met the man. He could be great and one hundred percent behind Archer, just like his wife was. For all we know, Archer is sweating over nothing."

Eden tapped her pencil on the pile of papers in front of her. She and her mother had been close, sharing secrets and dreams. But Eden hadn't known any of this. Her mother had come here to clear her head? When? Had her parents fought over the refuge? Her death had robbed them all of closure and healing. Where there had been happiness and merriment, now there was only anger and resentment. Her baby girls would never know the beauty of their grandmother's smile or her infectious laugh. It had been three years since her passing but sometimes Eden missed her so much, the pain was inescapable.

"Sorry. Too many television movies or epic family novels. You should have stopped me before I went overboard." She shook her head. "I should have said the name Monroe puts Archer on the defensive and left it at that." She laughed, her blue eyes inspecting Eden closely. "I'm thinking you're not a country girl?" Renata asked, reminding Eden where she was and what she was doing here.

"No, I'm not." Eden shook her head. What the hell was she doing? She had a plan, one that didn't need to get muddied by the unfounded speculation of a stranger. But Renata's words eased some of Eden's guilt over lying. Being Eden Caraway would make her job easier. And that was why she was here, period—to find justification to pull funding from Boone Ranch Refuge.

Renata seemed to be waiting for additional information—

"Renata?" Disapproval colored Archer's tone. Not as sharp as when he was speaking to his employees, but definitely not welcoming. "She's working. You're interrupting."

Archer seemed incapable of speaking to a human without condescension. But somehow, Renata didn't let it get to her.

"You caught me." Renata stood, holding up her hands in mock surrender. "I had to see the new recruit. People are talking, bets are being made, big brother."

Archer's blue eyes were glacial.

"Bets?" Eden asked, watching their interaction with interest. "What sort of bets?"

Renata glanced back and forth between them, smiling. "How long it'll be before he chases you off."

Archer continued to stare down his sister. "Is it too much to ask for a little professionalism, Renata?"

It was easy to empathize with him. His sister had come in and shared *far* too much information with her—a complete stranger. It was hard working with family. Even harder if one of them gets all chummy with the new employee, undermining authority. She knew *exactly* how that felt. Her brother, Greg, had tirelessly pursued Loretta, her first assistant. And once they'd gotten *close*, it hadn't been pleasant.

She took in the pinched look around Archer's blue eyes, the tightness bracketing his mouth, the posture that was anything but relaxed. Something about his stance resonated with her—a defensiveness, a vulnerability.

"Try?" One word, an order—and a plea. When he wasn't being rude, he had a very nice voice.

Eden slid her reading glasses on, using them to shield her inspection of the man. The man on paper was so different from the man in front of her. The man on paper was well-researched fact, and countless achievements. An academic with years of fieldwork and expertise. The man in front of her was broad and thick. Muscled yet lean, appearing more inclined to do the labor than study or research. Clearly he was capable of both. Which was something new. The men in her life were more likely to pick up a phone and call a repairman instead of picking up a hammer and making the repair themselves.

"Fine." Renata laughed. "I admit it, I heard about Fester and my curiosity was piqued."

Archer's blue eyes slammed into hers. He had piercing eyes that were…unnerving.

Hopefully he'd missed her thorough head-to-toe inspection. "What?" Her voice was tight and wary.

Archer shook his head, once.

"He didn't even *try* to bite you?" Renata was watching her just as closely.

Eden glanced back and forth between them. "He followed me." She shrugged. "And when I stopped, he'd push me forward with his nose." Whether or not that was relevant, she didn't know. Fester had seemed interested in her well-being. And after the initial fear had subsided, she'd appreciated his companionship.

"That's all?" Renata asked.

"He…he clicked his teeth at me," she mumbled.

Archer ran a hand over his face. "Clicked his teeth?"

"He did?" Renata's surprise was obvious.

She nodded. Clearly it meant something. "Is that bad?"

Archer crossed his arms over his chest and stared at her. The silence, and Archer's unflinching gaze, had her shifting in her chair. She hadn't done anything wrong. *I lied.* Well, not where the horse was concerned, so why did she feel guilty?

"What did you do?" Archer's voice was surprisingly soft. "When he clicked at you."

"I... I talked to him." She stared at the yellow invoice on the table.

"Talked to him?"

She glanced up at him. He seemed lost, working through some foreign concept or equation. When his gaze met hers again, his hostility was gone. But there was something equally unnerving in its place. Something warm and vibrant and heavy. She stared blindly at the papers in front of her.

Renata laughed. "I told you he's a woman's horse, Archer."

"No," Archer argued. "You're a woman. He bit you."

"Then maybe Fester has a crush." Renata tapped the table. "Which means you, Miss Caraway, just got yourself a horse."

Eden looked up then, startled. "Me?" That was the last thing she needed—more responsibility. Between her work, her family and her kids, she was shouldering enough. "No, thank you."

"She's teasing, Miss Caraway." Archer was using that soothing tone again, and it was having an odd effect on her.

"I am. You'll get used to it," Renata agreed.

"But now I have to run. Fisher and Kylee are finally going on a date and Tandy and I have twin duty. Can't be late. Knowing Fisher, he'll use it as an excuse to cancel—again. I know our brother so well."

Eden saw Archer's eye-roll, heard his mumbled, "It might help that you're his twin." She smiled before she could stop herself.

"You're probably right. You could come with me? Help with diaper duty and bath time?"

Archer's eyebrow arched sharply.

"Oh, come on Archer, if you could pretend your nephews were horses, you might actually like them—"

"I like them," Archer interrupted.

"I know." Renata pressed a kiss to his cheek. "You love us all, even if we drive you crazy." She waved at Eden. "Nice to meet you, Eden."

"You, too," she answered.

Archer stayed where he was, his gaze sweeping the room. "Progress?"

"I think so." She patted the four stacks she'd made, color-tabbed and neatly clipped, with accounting tapes affixed to the front.

"It's almost eight." He glanced at her.

"It is?" She looked around. No clock. "I had no idea."

"Where are you staying?" he asked.

"The Lodge." She met his gaze. "Since there is no time to waste, it made sense to stay close."

"I can drive you." It wasn't an offer, it was a statement. Considering she had no way to get there, there was no point in arguing with him. Even if something deep inside her chest protested.

"Thank you," she said, collecting her things—sliding his file between two packets—and tucking it all back into her briefcase.

He nodded, his expression rigid, and studied her. And while his gaze made her feel wobbly and unsteady, she had no idea how to read Dr. Archer Boone.

Archer held the door open for her. She was limping as she stepped out onto the front porch. "You hurt?"

"Didn't have the best hiking shoes." She stopped at the edge of the porch, gripped the porch rail and took a deep breath. "It's cool. I hadn't expected that."

Her hair was slipping from the clip on the back of her head; one long strand blew in the breeze. He cleared his throat, that peculiar tightening pressing in on him again.

"Where is home for you?" He knew nothing about this woman except he was paying her very well for her time and expertise. And that he seemed to be allergic to her—perhaps it was her perfume? Whatever it was, his throat seemed to tighten whenever he was close to her.

"Houston," she said. "Crisp evenings are a rarity."

"Clear night," he said, looking up. With the sun almost gone, the navy and black bled into the pale horizon. Overhead, the sky was already sparkling. Among the chirp of the crickets, the *who-who* of an owl rang out. "Hear that?" he asked.

She looked at him, eyebrow cocked in question.

"An owl." He nodded into the dark but watched her.

She closed her eyes, perfectly still. She was listening, a line forming between her brows and her lips parting.

Eden Caraway was…odd. In his experience, women talked. Too much. But Eden didn't volunteer information or reveal what she was thinking. She was reserved in a way that unnerved him. Her features were controlled, her voice neutral, yet she didn't shy away from eye contact. But now, the slight flicker, some hint of an unchecked response, piqued his interest.

Her smile was disconcerting. It grew, erasing the furrow from her brow and bringing her to life. When her eyes opened, met his, his throat grew tight and his lungs empty.

"I hear it." She stared out into the dark, leaning forward on the rail. When she looked up, she gasped. "So many stars." Her whisper was so faint he wasn't sure he'd heard her. She brushed past him, descending the stairs to stand and stare up at the night sky overhead.

He frowned, forcing his attention elsewhere. It was late and he was tired. His curiosity was solely because she was new— nothing more. The fact that she was here to help ensure his success most likely played a part in it, as well. He didn't like relying on others. His motto, If You Want Something Done Right, Do It Yourself, served him well in life. But he had to put some trust in this unusual woman. Perhaps the fact that she was so attractive was the problem.

He cleared his throat.

Apparently he wasn't the only one who had noticed. His cousin Toben was already making plans to show the temp a good time with a cowboy. He glanced at Miss Caraway… Eden, hoping she wasn't interested in having a good time with his cousin—or any man, for that matter. He needed her undivided attention and time.

"Is that Fester?" Eden asked, pointing.

Sure enough, Fester was at the fence, head up, ears pricked forward, nickering sweetly— at Eden. He glanced at the woman, then the horse. "He's talking to you."

She looked at him. "How do you know?"

"Animals communicate just as clearly as people," he said. "More so. There's not as much room for misinterpretation. A horse nickers, he's saying 'Come talk to me.' He snorts or blows, he's excited—"

"What if he…if he sort of…" She glanced at him. "Hugged me?"

Archer looked at her. "What do you mean?"

"I… I caught my shoe between a couple of rocks so I stopped to free it… He stepped close so his chin was on the back of my shoulder and leaned his head against mine." She used her hand and arm to clarify as she was talking.

"He did?" Archer sighed, pleased and frustrated at the same time.

She nodded.

"And he followed you back? Behind you?" he asked.

She nodded again. "It might sound strange, but I think he was watching over me."

"Not strange," Archer argued. "Intuitive. He was watching over you."

Fester kept up the nickering, tossing his head a little.

"May I?" she asked.

Archer nodded, walking down the fence line to turn on a few lights. He hung back, curious to see the exchange between Fester and the only human the horse had acknowledged favorably.

"Should I do anything?" She glanced back at him, hesitating.

"No," Archer said. "There's a fence between you. He just wants you close."

"Do you?" she asked Fester, her voice soft and calm—not high-pitched or affected but inviting and warm.

Fester stretched his head out, and Eden stepped closer.

Archer was in shock. Not only did Fester clearly adore the woman, Eden seemed to understand exactly what Fester needed. She didn't reach for him, she simply stood and let the horse nicker and blow against her chest and neck. She didn't try to touch his nose or rub the horse's face. She might not realize that was significant, but he did. A person didn't like a stranger touching their face. Neither did most horses. Somehow, Eden Caraway understood that.

"Hi," she said softly. "Thank you for walking me here."

Archer draped his arm on the top rail of the wooden fence, resting his chin. What the hell? Maybe Renata was right? Maybe Fester recognized something in Eden that brought him pleasure. Whatever it was, it made him happy to see Fester so content. This was what he wanted for all the horses that came through the refuge. A sense of comfort and belonging.

The shrill chirp of a cell phone split the night. Fester jerked his head back, his chin clipping the side of Eden's head as the horse startled.

"Are you okay?" Archer asked, instantly at her side.

"I'm fine." She was rubbing her head. "It's not his fault." She pressed her hand to her forehead. "It spooked me, too."

He liked the way she defended Fester. "We should probably get you some ice. Just in case."

"I'm fine," she argued, waving him away before she pulled her cell phone from her pocket. "Yes?" she answered.

Archer stared at her. She'd dismissed him.

"When did this happen?" There was no sign of the calm and controlled Eden Caraway now. "He just left?" Her tone was razor-edged as she stalked the length of the fence. "I can't... Oh, Clara."

He saw her shoulders droop. Saw Fester clop down the fence line to nicker at her.

"No, of course. We'll make it work. I'll book the first flight out tomorrow. Give them kisses for me, Clara." She hung up the phone, leaning her head against Fester's broad nose without thought.

"There a problem?" he asked, bracing himself. He'd do whatever he could to make her stay. He needed her help.

"No." She collected herself, her posture stiffening and her voice deadpan once more. "No problem at all. I do, however, need to get to the Lodge. I have some personal business to attend to."

Archer nodded. "Nothing that will interfere with your work, I hope?" If he sounded callous, it wasn't intentional.

She shook her head, not bothering to make

eye contact as she brushed past him. "Not at all."

He sighed, relief washing over him. She was staying, and he would be ready to convince Mr. Monroe that his continued support of the refuge was essential for expansion. "I'll take you to the Lodge," he said, the weight of his deadline easing for the first time since he'd received Monroe's letter.

Chapter 3

Eden finished scanning the invoices for the first quarter and set to work color-coding the tabs on the spreadsheet she was creating. She liked having everything in one place, no back and forth, riffling through things for backup or verification. After tossing and turning in her bed all night, she appreciated the distraction her work was giving her. If she didn't have something to do, she was likely to call Clark and rip into him for what he'd done.

Did Ivy understand her father had broken his word—again? No. She was too young to know. Eden hoped. But Eden knew. This wasn't the first time Clark had been sent on some "emergency" trip that conveniently fell on the week he'd demanded for his visitation. This wasn't the first time Clark had promised Ivy all sorts of adventures and fun and time only to take off before any of his promises were fulfilled. This wasn't the first time she'd been forced to adjust her schedule even after she'd been assured that he had everything under control and that she should relax.

Thank God for Clara.

Clara, Ivy and baby Lily would be here soon. The suite at the Lodge would work, putting them all in one large room for the remainder of her stay. The rental car company had upgraded her sedan to a minivan so Clara and the girls weren't stuck in the Lodge all day. As pissed as she was at Clark, she was equally delighted that the girls were coming. She hated being parted from them. Lily was still so small, just seven months old. The thought of missing out on a milestone— rolling over, laughs, funny faces—was too much for her. And Ivy, her wide-eyed ray of light, made her look forward to coming home all day, every day.

"Coffee?" Archer placed a large cup of black coffee on the corner of the table.

Eden glanced at the cup, then the man she'd decided to avoid as much as possible.

It wasn't just that she'd had a surprisingly intimate dream about him. But even awake, she had to accept that she was attracted to him. And while Archer Boone seemed clueless to pretty much everything that wasn't horse-related, she'd be mortified if he caught her ogling his angular jaw or intense eyes or firm thighs. And his butt. Nicely showcased in his well-worn, work-faded jeans.

"No?" he asked, reaching for the cup.

He was standing right there. *Stop thinking about his body.* "Thank you." She was so startled that she grabbed the handle and took a sip, scalding the roof of her mouth in the process.

"It's hot," he said.

She nodded, setting the cup down to cover her mouth. "Yes, it sure is," she mumbled, her words garbled.

"I came to get you this morning, but you were already gone." There was a hint of accusation.

"The airline delivered my bags to the Lodge while I was working yesterday." She pointed at the tennis shoes sitting side by side against the wall. "I walked."

"Just make sure there's no scorpions in them before you put them on." He sipped his coffee, his gaze fixed on hers. "They tend to climb all the way inside to rest."

"Good to know." She glanced at her tennis shoes and wondered if they were already inhabited.

"Miss Caraway, do you have an assignment after this one?"

She was no longer thinking about scorpions. "What do you have in mind?"

"I could use a bookkeeper." He nodded at the box on the table and the two still waiting for her attention on the floor at her feet.

"You could," she agreed. "But—"

"There would be more to it," he cut her off. "I'd like you to work with Fester."

She gripped the mug in her hands, slowly turning it in a circle. "I have no experience with horses, Dr. Boone."

"Archer." He ran a hand over his face and sat in the chair opposite her. "I know you've never worked with animals before. There'd be a learning curve. But you're smart, your eyes…" He stopped, clearing his throat and taking a sip of his coffee before trying again. "You're smart. Fester seems to respond favorably to you on his own. That's a start—I assure you. But I can show you a few things that might help. Just until I can determine what he wants and needs."

She sat back, her mug forgotten. What about her eyes? Nope, she didn't care a thing about what he thought of her eyes. "You and Fester aren't close?"

He sat forward, resting his elbows on his knees. "No, ma'am, we are not. He barely tolerates me, but he knows I'm the one with the food. I admit, he fascinates me. I'm an animal behaviorist, Miss Caraway, so studying and learning an animal's...bonds are important. You and Fester have a connection—something he's had with no human since he came to us five months ago. I'd like you to help him find his place here, his herd. And I'd like to study the process."

She met his gaze. He was sincere. And intense. She drew in an unsteady breath. "I can't. Thank you."

"Can't isn't a philosophy I subscribe to, Miss Caraway."

She bit back a smile. She appreciated his determination. But he wouldn't feel the same when she was a Monroe again. "Dr. Boone, I'm afraid things might get a bit more complicated."

He frowned. "Why?"

Because I'm lying to you about who I am.
She swallowed, choosing another truth. "My
children are arriving today."

His frown increased. "Children?" His surprise was obvious.

She nodded. "I have two."

His frown sharpened, his cup spinning in
his hands. He opened his mouth, closed it,
then said, "Surely your husband—"

"My personal life is my own, Dr. Boone."
She straightened in her chair. "I informed you
only so you'd understand my answer to your
offer."

He continued staring at her, frowning.

He could frown all he wanted; she wasn't
going to change her mind or apologize for having children, for crying out loud. Besides, she
couldn't stay. She wasn't here to help him…
she was here for her father.

The review board meeting was in two
weeks. And in those two weeks' time Eden had
to have the information that would allow her to
support her father's wishes. Once she'd gained
his support, she'd be out of her basement cu-
bicle and into her father's good graces—where
she belonged. Something she'd been far more

enthusiastic about before meeting Archer Boone, his sister and Fester.

"I apologize for prying." Archer's gaze was no less intense, but his frown had faded into something softer, something vulnerable and searching.

"No apologies necessary." Her voice wavered. He needed to stop looking at her like that. She needed to keep a level head. "Isn't there some sort of specialist that can see Fester? Surely there are people far more qualified who could help him."

He sat back, stretching his long legs out in front of him and crossing them at the ankles. "There are, but he didn't respond well to the two who visited." His smile was tight. "One went home with a horse bite bruise on his thigh. The other said Fester should be turned out to pasture. Or destroyed." He shook his head, his attention wandering out the window. "He's too young, too spirited, to be written off. I've seen the damage that a horse can cause, but… I'm not ready to give up on him." He spoke carefully, as if his mind was already searching for possibilities.

Eden stared; she couldn't help it. He was lost in thought, determined to find an answer. What she wouldn't give to hear his thoughts out loud. He wanted to help Fester, wanted the *animal* to be happy. He cared, deeply. Yes, he was a little rough around the edges, but he was direct—not rude necessarily. And he was incredibly handsome. So far everything she'd learned of the unexpected Dr. Boone was good. Which, considering her purpose, was bad. It would be easier if he'd been flagrantly misspending grant funds or his work ethic was suspect or his facility was dangerous or out of compliance. None of which was the case. Worse, she found herself respecting his single-minded, detail-oriented, fiery loyalty to his work.

If he ever used that undivided focus on a woman… She shivered, snippets of her dream all too vivid. The shudder that ran along her spine was unexpectedly delightful. *No no no.* She needed more coffee. Or a long run. Or something. Why her mind kept detouring into the bedroom when it came to Archer Boone was a complete mystery.

"Problem is, he won't work with anyone." His gaze locked with hers. "He pretends people don't exist…" The unspoken "except you" hung in the air.

Eden refused to take the bait. What he wanted was impossible. Besides, the Fester

Archer spoke of wasn't the same horse who'd walked her home and hugged her. Her Fester had taken care of her, sought out her company, talked to her. She couldn't believe she was the only one Fester would warm up to.

"Just like a child, Dr. Boone," Eden murmured, focusing on her papers before she changed her mind about helping Archer with his wayward horse. "Keep them busy and they stay out of trouble. Leave them idle and that's when the trouble starts."

"Exactly. And it's Archer. Fester has been through a lot, Miss Caraway." Archer stood, slapping his cowboy hat against his thigh. He paced from the window and back before stopping directly in front of her.

"I'm sure you'll find someone to help you."

"I've tried." He shook his head. "I'm disappointed you won't help me."

She looked up then, frustrated by his choice of words. It would be easier to say no if it was *just* a job. But to Archer, this was so much more. "I'm an accountant, Dr. Boone. *That* is my job. And considering how little time I have left here, I should probably concentrate on the job you hired me for." Her fingers fell to the turquoise stones, seeking calm. *Keep it together.* She had legitimate reasons to feel guilty. Turning down his request to help with a difficult horse wasn't one of them.

He stared at her for some time. His pale gaze drifted, traveling over her face, her hair and her neck. His attention lingered there. And Eden sat frozen, her skin going warm.

He cleared his throat and nodded, leveling an almost hostile glare at the piles in front of her. "You do that, Miss Caraway," he bit out, slapping his hat against his thigh again, making her jump. He leveled a hard stare at her and left, slamming the door behind him.

She sat, stunned. All that because she'd said no? Looks be damned, his temperament was no better than Fester's. She already had two children; she didn't need more.

She stood, carrying her coffee mug to the small break room down the hall. She added a heaping amount of sugar and creamer before heading back to her office. She lingered over the pictures that lined the hall. Newspaper clippings, magazine articles, ads, fliers, programs and several certificates honoring Dr. Boone, the refuge and the important work being done here.

Several of the refuge horses had gone on to help out as therapy animals, some were companion animals, while others stayed right here, working on the ranch. Her guilt increased. She knew the refuge would probably survive without the grant funds, but they'd likely mean cuts. Cuts for the horses, like Fester. Or Archer's staff... She tore her attention from the wall and returned to her desk.

What did her father know that she didn't?

She sighed, rolling her neck and sipping her coffee. She placed the mug on the edge of the desk and moved to the window. Constant motion. Man, dogs, horses and some cattle. No one was idle or hesitant about what needed to be done.

There was one large barn that fed into a series of open sheds, made up of stalls. At the end of the sheds, smaller pens branched off. Some looked like small tracks with a large wheel in the middle. Others resembled small mazes, with chutes and gates. Like the ranch archway, the structures were made of thick beams and stone. While functionality clearly took priority, there was no denying the buildings blended seamlessly into their surroundings—in harmony with one another.

Archer strode toward a long open shed with several stalls, on a mission. He paused, smiling at the small gray-and-black dog following at his side. The dog barked, circling

Archer, his stubby tail wagging in obvious excitement. Archer laughed, his smile easy—and beautiful. There was a sudden tug in her chest, a long-forgotten ache.

She turned back to her work. Time wasn't going to wait for her to recover from her momentary weakness. Archer Boone may be handsome and oddly fascinating; he was also firmly in the no-go zone. Considering she was lying to him about who she was and what she was doing here, the chances of them having any interaction once she'd left were slight to say the least.

But his refuge, his work and the good he did was—as far as she could tell—irrefutable. He was no-kill, finding homes for those he could and keeping those he couldn't. He rehabilitated not only the animals' bodies, but their spirits. Not to mention the wildlife he'd taken in and relocated. From an injured bobcat and a red-tailed hawk unable to fly to a three-legged deer, Archer was hell-bent on taking care of them. And his paperwork, as disorganized as it was, offered no red flags.

Her mother had always championed the refuge. When review time had rolled around, she'd believed in the refuge's vision and fought to support it. And if Renata was right and she really meant to create an endowment for the refuge, how could Eden play a part in ending that?

What was her father's real motivation?

She had so many questions. And no answers.

Bottom line, the questions shouldn't matter. She had to find something to take before the board to substantiate all the reasons Boone Ranch Refuge should not be awarded funds. Even if she was beginning to have doubts.

Archer glanced back at the refuge administrative building again. The stone building rested on a slight butte over the rest of the refuge. He'd put it there so, even on those rare days he was trapped at his desk, he could see what was happening outside.

Now he was outside, staring at the building. For the six or seventh time this morning.

She'd said no.

He'd laid it out there, told her he needed her—Fester needed her. And she'd said no.

He was angry. And disappointed.

The crunch of gravel drew his attention to his cousins, Deacon and Toben.

"Hey, Archer." Deacon sauntered up, his

hat tipped forward on his brow. "That little roan that came in yesterday? She's coughing."

"She's isolated?" he asked.

"The four of them won't separate," Toben said.

Deacon shrugged. "We tried, but we figured—since they've been together this long—parting them would upset them."

It was the right thing to do. If one was sick, they were likely all sick, so he'd treat them all. They were in sad shape. "Are they still in the south holding pen?"

Deacon nodded.

"I'll head there now."

"She's a pretty little thing." Toben's voice was unexpectedly soft.

Archer smiled. "Once we get her healthy, she's yours." It was important for the staff to connect to the horses. Horses were social animals, and highly intuitive. If they knew a human loved them, it boosted their confidence. And these horses needed a whole lot of support right now.

Toben laughed. "I wasn't talking about the roan, Archer." He shook his head. "I'd be hard-pressed to keep a clear head with something that soft and sweet working next door."

"You need to find a hobby that doesn't involve skirt-chasing," Deacon snapped.

Archer followed his gaze to find Eden Caraway standing on the front porch of the administrative office. She stretched, arching her back before leaning forward on the porch railing.

Archer scowled. She should be working, not distracting his staff. He agreed with Deacon. Toben couldn't keep a clear head around any attractive woman—which was, as far as Archer was concerned, Toben's greatest weakness. Women were just people. And Eden Caraway was…just a woman. He cleared his throat, grappling with the effect this woman had on him. He frowned, tugging at his shirt collar and focusing on his anger instead of the curve of her neck or the swell of soft curves he found all too distracting.

Fester whinnied.

"Damn." Deacon sighed. "That horse has got it bad. Pretty sure he's stayed penned because of her."

Archer agreed, watching the large black horse with interest. Fester was doing everything in his power to grab Eden's attention, prancing along the fence line, nickering, whinnying. He smiled in spite of himself.

"Look at that," Toben murmured, equally impressed with Fester's little display.

His irritation flared. Poor Fester. He had no idea his affection was one-sided. But Archer did, and he was sad for the horse. And fuming. Eden had no idea what a gift Fester was giving her. "Too bad Miss Caraway doesn't seem to care about Fester."

"I wouldn't be so sure about that," Deacon said.

Archer froze, glancing back at Fester. Eden had made her way, smiling, to where Fester waited at the fence. When she was close enough, she held her hand out, letting Fester blow and nuzzle it. She moved forward then, standing on the fence so she could rest her arms along the top beam.

"He's just eating it up," Toben said. "Wonder what she's saying."

Fester nudged Eden's clip from her hair, letting her long hair fall around her shoulders. Archer watched, a strange tightness pressing in on his chest. She laughed, the sound ringing out and stirring a flare of hope in Archer's chest.

"You should talk to her about—"

"Miss Caraway is here to get the books in shape. Then she'll be on her way." His words were a reminder. It didn't make sense to be hopeful when it came to this woman. She had her own life, one that had no room for him—or his horses.

"When are you heading in to the hospital?" Toben asked.

Archer sighed. He worked part-time at the local veterinary teaching hospital. His extensive experience with exotic animals made him the resident expert on everything that wasn't a cat or dog. "Shortly."

His current patient, a poisoned cockatoo, was almost recovered, his feathers returning to their normal bright white. But the bird was finicky about being handled and seemed to tolerate Archer best when it came to taking his meds.

He also needed to confirm that Mrs. Ballencier was bringing in the lion cub she'd inherited from some eccentric uncle. He wanted to convince her that finding the cub a permanent home—one prepared to accommodate the size and needs of a full-grown male lion—was her only option.

As much as he enjoyed cases that offered him a challenge, there were times he'd gladly resign his position to work full-time at the refuge. This was where his heart was.

But Toben's question wasn't about Archer's responsibility to the vet hospital. He suspected it had to do with Eden Caraway. Once Archer was off premises, Toben wouldn't have anyone intercepting his attempts to charm the woman.

"She's leaving next week." Archer shot his cousin a look.

Deacon groaned. "Don't make her more appealing than she already is."

Toben's laugh grated on Archer's nerves.

"You know she's an actual person? Here for work?" He glanced at the woman carrying on a conversation with Fester. "It is possible she has no interest in you."

"It's possible. But highly unlikely." Toben nudged Archer, winking.

Archer glared at him.

"Oh, come on, Archer. Just because you're a monk doesn't mean the rest of us are." Toben shook his head. "You're gonna have a hell of a time catching up to your brothers if you don't get to work soon."

Archer's glare didn't waver until Toben had disappeared around the end of the shed.

"He's a dick," Deacon said, clapping Archer on the shoulder.

Archer nodded at his cousin. Deacon had

lost his wife and daughters in a car crash two years before. Since then, he'd been wandering, working a few months here and there, helping Archer when he felt the need to plant roots. Unlike Toben, Deacon kept to himself, stayed out of trouble and had a way with horses. Archer understood Deacon, liked him. Unlike Toben.

But he *understood* few people. That included the rest of his family. He didn't need anyone telling him what to do with his life. If, and it was a big if, he ever found a woman who sparked his interest—romantically— there was no guarantee he'd want children. He knew his limitations. A wife, children, emotional entanglements, were things he had a hard time imagining in his future. He was fine as he was.

Lucky barked, drawing Archer's attention.

He glanced down at the dog's eager expression. "You can bite him," Archer offered. "He may be family, but his head is firmly up his ass."

Deacon laughed as he made his way back up the fence line to the hay barn.

Lucky's stubby tail wagged frantically, drawing a smile from Archer. Lucky was a good dog. Technically, Lucky was his brother

Fisher's dog. But Lucky had decided the whole ranch was his home. A month ago, Archer had woken to Lucky scratching on the front door of his cabin. They'd enjoyed their breakfast together on the front porch, and the dog had been at his heels ever since.

Lucky barked, peering around Archer to stare at the entrance to the refuge. A blue minivan came bouncing along the road, kicking up a steady stream of red dust in its wake. When the vehicle turned under the arch, he expected it to turn around—most people wound up here by accident. Instead, the vehicle pulled up to the administrative office and parked. Archer headed toward the van, hoping it wasn't some salesman.

"Clara?" There was no denying the relief in Eden's voice. Archer waited, watching her cross the yard—leaving Fester with ears twitching and his head high—toward the minivan.

"Eden." A woman slipped from the car and they hugged. "What a journey. Your little misses have been such troupers, though. All smiles and sweetness, like their mother."

Eden smiled sadly. "I'm so sorry you had to make the trip alone. There are times I think

I should drag him back to court for sole custody."

Archer watched; Eden's frustration was unmistakable.

"Don't fret now, we're here." The older woman squeezed her shoulders. "Your little misses are tickled to be back with their momma."

The van door opened and a giggle of pure delight floated out. Lucky whimpered, running around Archer's legs in circles as the giggling went on.

Eden was smiling. So beautiful. So...sweet.

Archer blew out a deep breath, grappling with a strange tightness in his chest.

"Did you miss me?" she asked, reaching into the minivan. Minutes later she emerged with a curly-haired girl in her arms.

"Mommy," the little girl cooed, hugging Eden as if her life depended on it. "Mommy."

"I've got you," Eden said. "Did you ride on a big airplane?"

The little girl nodded, still holding her tightly.

"Where are we?" the little girl asked.

"We are...we are on a horse ranch," Eden said.

"We staying here?" the little girl asked.

"No, no, Ivy," the other woman said. "We will stay in the big house on the hill."

"Do you want to see the horses?" Eden asked.

The girl nodded, smiling.

Archer had only nephews. So this tiny golden girl was oddly captivating. And when she reached out toward the fence where Fester stood, his heart thudded against his ribs. She was fragile and delicate, even if her excitement and energy made her ten times bigger. But when Eden carried her daughter in the direction of Fester, Archer blocked her path. "Miss Caraway…" His voice faded to a stop as two pairs of light hazel eyes regarded him steadily.

"Who that?" the little girl asked, smiling broadly.

"This is Dr. Boone, Ivy. Dr. Boone, this is my daughter Ivy." She shifted the little girl, smiling that bone-melting smile at her daughter.

"We seeing the horses," Ivy said. "Wanna come?"

Archer glanced at the little girl. Resisting Ivy's enthusiasm was a challenge. She was adorable. But the smile on his face tightened

when he thought of Ivy's little fingers anywhere close to Fester's mouth.

A cry came from the minivan, drawing all
eyes—and a high-pitched whinny from Fester.

"Lily's wake," Ivy announced. "My baby."

"Baby?" Archer repeated.

"My other daughter, Lily," Eden explained.

Other daughter. Her words came back to
him then. She had two. He'd heard the custody comment. So Eden Caraway was divorced and the girls' father wasn't carrying
his weight. Which helped explain why she
had no time for anything else.

"Pretty horsey." Ivy clapped.

Fester whinnied again, prancing along the
fence line. Big, powerful and far too dangerous for Ivy. "Now is not the time, Miss Caraway. I suggest you take your lunch break and
help settle your children at the Lodge."

Miss Caraway's eyes widened. "I appreciate your concern, Dr. Boone—"

"Good," he said. "Let me make this clear.
Unless I am with them, your daughters need
to stay away from the horses. Especially Fester. Is that understood?"

She blinked but didn't say a word. Ivy was
frowning, tears welling up in her big eyes.

"He mad, Momma?" Ivy whispered.

"No, no, Ivy. He wants to keep you safe." Eden's voice was soft and cajoling.

Archer didn't miss the lethal glare Eden shot his way before she headed back to the minivan.

Her anger wasn't important. He was her boss—his place, his rules. For the time being, he needed her. Maybe Eden was right—keeping her around would be complicated. And yet Fester wanted her. And maybe that was enough to figure out how to uncomplicate things.

He glanced at Eden. Ivy stared back at him over Eden's shoulder. Her golden curls danced on the breeze, her huge hazel eyes unblinking. Ivy waved, her tiny fingers splayed wide even as her chin quivered. He was an asshole. Yes, he'd been trying to keep Eden's charming daughter at a safe distance. But he'd never meant to make the little girl cry. A little girl who kept waving.

So he waved back.

Her smile was so bright, he had no choice but to smile in return.

He sighed, watching Eden climb into the minivan, and the van bounce down the drive. He'd stay out of Eden's way, and he'd do his best to stay away from her and her children. He didn't know much about people and relationships. But work, he knew. Best course of action—work.

Chapter 4

Eden held Ivy's hand as she reached for Lily's car seat handle. While Ivy was fully recovered from her disappointment with the horses, Eden was fuming. She would never, ever put her daughter in jeopardy. She had no illusions about Fester. He might be partial to her, but she wouldn't assume the same affection applied to her daughter.

Archer's warning plucked at a wound he had nothing to do with. A wound that, no matter how hard she tried to forget, stayed irritated and raw. Her children were her everything. And she did the best she could to be a good, hands-on mother. Even if her father, brother and Clark were all too eager to point out her inadequacies.

She was so busy stewing over her encounter with Archer that she didn't see a strange man coming out of one of the Lodge doors. Until she'd run into him.

His hands clasped her shoulders. "You all right?" he asked. "Shoulda been lookin' at where I was going—" But his words broke off as he stared at her. And the expression on the older man's face made her pause. "Who do we have here?" he asked.

She was torn between embarrassment and curiosity herself. "Eden Caraway," she said. "I'm a guest here. These are my daughters, Ivy—"

"That's me," Ivy said, smiling up at the man. "This is Lily."

The older man stooped, shaking Ivy's hand before peering into Lily's car seat. "Well, it's nice to meet you, little lady. And your sister, too." He straightened, leveling her with deep blue eyes. "There's no denying you're their momma. I'm Teddy Boone."

Mrs. Monroe only visited twice, but she cared about this place, my father... Eden hadn't missed the specific mention of Renata's father.

"Eden Caraway, was it?" he asked, his eyes narrowing slightly. "Guess Jenny checked you in?"

She nodded. "Yes. Nice to meet you, Mr. Boone. You've an amazing place here. The whole ranch."

"Wait, now," he said, crossing his arms over his chest. "You're the one helping out my son, Archer?"

"Yes, sir," she murmured, trying not to let the mere mention of Archer's name stoke her fading anger.

He grinned. "Don't envy you that task, Miss Caraway." He placed an odd inflection on her last name. "My son can be a might prickly now and then. And more than a might particular."

"I'll survive the week," she answered.

"Miss Eden." Clara joined them. "Let me take Lily."

"Let me help," Teddy offered. "I've enough grandbabies to know those things weigh more than they should."

Eden smiled, relinquishing the car seat to the handsome older man. But the look that passed between Clara and Teddy caught Eden's full attention. And, boy, was it a look. Clara's blush, the way she averted her brown eyes, made Eden stop and stare. And Teddy Boone's smile was slow and surprised, in a pleasant way.

"And all you lovely ladies are staying in the suite, I'm thinking?" Teddy asked.

"Saweet?" Ivy repeated. "Like candy?"

Eden and Clara laughed. "It's a fancy name for a big bedroom," Eden explained. "Big enough for you and me, Lily, and Clara, too."

"Clara?" Teddy asked, offering his free hand. "Teddy Boone. Nice to meet you, ma'am."

Clara smiled. "And you."

Eden led Ivy to their suite, trying not to watch the beyond-adorable play between Clara and Teddy Boone. If Clara had a little cowboy romance, good for her. She'd lost her husband years ago. Clara's only remaining family was right here, even if they weren't blood.

"Mr. Boone," Eden said. "Clara takes care of the girls while I'm working. Would you mind showing her around? Is that all right, Clara? I can spend my lunchtime with the girls."

Clara shot her a wide-eyed a look, but Eden just smiled.

"I'd be delighted. I'm thinking you'll need

access to the washer and dryer." Teddy placed Lily's car seat on the bed. "You feel free to use the family kitchen while you're here. We have a big ol' fancy one the staff uses for the guests staying here, but it's always hopping busy." He led Clara from the room, still talking.

Eden slipped Lily from the car seat and smiled at her baby. "How are you? Wet, I'll bet."

While Eden changed her daughter's diaper, Ivy bounced on one of the big beds. "Momma," she said between bounces. "I can see the whole world."

Eden was just finishing Lily's diaper. She followed her bouncing daughter's gaze out the window. She'd been too preoccupied to stop and appreciate the view before now. And what a view. Hills stretched as far as the eye could see, a veritable patchwork of green and tan pastures and fields. Towering trees, the glimpse of a river and a handful of roofs—about as country as country could get. And the sky. She stared out the window at the fluffy white clouds and pale blue sky. So blue, clear and never ending.

"It does look like it, doesn't it?" Eden said,

cradling Lily close and walking to the window. She and Ivy counted five windmills, eight horses and a bunch of cows. Overall, it was a peaceful view, meant for enjoying from the wide deck that extended along the house. If she had time, that's just what she'd do. "What do you think, Lily?"

Lily's curls brushed Eden's chin as she turned her bright gaze out the window. "Na-na-na," Lily said, waving one fist.

"Ivy?" Eden asked.

Ivy liked to interpret all of her little sister's yammering. "She likes it." She went back to bouncing then.

Eden smiled. "After I get done working, we can go walking. Maybe Mr. Boone will take us exploring?"

"Be happy to," Mr. Boone said from the doorway. "Might just hitch up the wagon for your little ladies."

"I don't want to put you out. We can just go for a walk?" Eden offered, wincing as Lily tugged a handful of her hair. "It'll help wear Ivy out."

He smiled at Lily. "We can do that, too."

Lily reached for him, cooing in delight.

"May I?" he asked.

She nodded. "Thank you, Mr. Boone."

"Can I make you some lunch?" Clara asked her.

She shook her head. "I'm fine. But I should head back so I don't upset Dr. Boone. Any more than I already have," she added, mumbling.

"Don't let my boy to get you, Miss Caraway. He's not real good with people, but he's a good man. That I know." Teddy was bouncing Lily on his hip, who was giggling.

"You're very good with babies, Mr. Boone," Clara observed.

"I've got a whole passel of grandbabies, Miss Clara. All boys, though. I admit, they're my joy." He made a silly face at Lily.

My joy… Unlike her own father. The words tugged at her heart. Ivy and Lily were his only grandchildren. Maybe it was his new, needy young wife. Or the fact that Eden, and her daughters, looked like her mother. Whatever it was, her father seemed all too eager to keep Eden and her daughters at arm's length. He took care of them financially, assuring her she would never make as much working for anyone else. Whether that was true or not, she never worried about keeping a roof over her head or paying her bills. And that, she supposed, was some sort of devotion.

But if she didn't have Clara, she'd have no one to smile with, to savor the girls' growth with. At times, she ached for more. For love, touch, a father for her girls, someone to love them all.

"Miss Caraway?" Mr. Boone was speaking. "You okay?"

She nodded. "Eden, please."

"Mr. Boone was offering to pack up a lunch for you and Dr. Boone. We'll bring it down later," Clara said.

"I'm not sure he wants the girls in the way," Eden said.

Teddy Boone chuckled. "You both need to eat, don't ya? You let me worry about Archer."

"I appreciate the offer, Mr. Boone, but we'll be fine. *Really.*" She stressed the last word, hoping he'd listen. She didn't want another run-in with Archer Boone. She'd rather not see him again today, or she might say something she'd regret.

Minutes later, Eden was riding back to the refuge with Toben.

"Good thing Uncle Teddy gave me a call," Toben said as they bounced along the dirt road. "Archer's been spitting nails since you left."

Eden scowled out the front window, saying only, "It's illegal to have employees work through lunch." He was the one who had told her to take a lunch. Now he was being ridiculous. More than ridiculous. She'd been gone for half an hour, tops. She was more than ready to "spit nails" right back at him. She'd love to knock that chip right off his shoulder. What would he do if she told him she was a Monroe? She was tempted, more than tempted.

"And Fester's been pitching a fit since you left," Toben explained. "Reared up at Archer, charged him and jumped the fence—took off."

Eden stared at Toben then. "He did?" Poor Fester. And…poor Archer. He was upset over the horse—not her.

Toben nodded, a dimple appearing in his cheek. "Seems I'm not the only one who's interested in you, Miss Caraway."

Eden ignored Toben's attempt to flirt, worried over Fester. No one wanted a mean horse—especially one so big and aggressive. What would happen to him?

And there was Archer. Whether or not Fester had managed to physically injure Archer, she suspected the blow to his pride would hurt more. Gruff temperament aside, there was no denying the man wanted only what was best for the horses. And an animal like Fester would be a puzzle Archer couldn't give up on.

Archer sat in the saddle, letting his horse, River, lead the other horses out into the lower pasture. This group was headed to auction in a few weeks—strong, healthy and ready for a home. Until then, they'd be happy here. The water tank was full, there were tall shade trees, and he'd made sure there were mineral and salt blocks in the two troughs at either side of the pasture.

River picked up speed along the creek. Archer sighed, letting the horse run through the water once, then twice, pawing at the water with his front hooves. He'd always loved the water—that's how he'd earned his name. And on a hot day like today, Archer didn't mind a refreshing dousing in the creek.

They rode back to the refuge dripping wet.

"River get hot?" Renata said with a laugh, stepping back when he slipped from his saddle.

"We both were," Archer agreed, shaking water from his head.

"Any sign of Fester?" she asked. "Toben told me."

He shook his head. "He'll come back when he's hungry." He sighed.

"Dad left some food in your office." She nudged him. "Said he needed to talk to you."

Archer looked at his sister. "About what?"

She shrugged. "He didn't say. Thought I'd try out a few of the new rides for the parade. If that's okay. Toben said you've got a few sweet horses to choose from. He thought the dapple and the blue mare would be good choices."

He nodded. "I've been thinking the mare might be a good fit for Shawn. He's ready for his own horse, and she's about as even-footed and responsive as a horse can be."

"What's Fisher say?" Renata asked.

"I need Fisher's permission?" Archer asked, frowning at his sister.

Renata laughed. "Well, considering Shawn is his brother-in-law and Fisher and Kylee have baby twins to keep them busy, yes. I think you might want to make sure they want Shawn to have a horse. On top of everything else."

Archer shook his head. "I'd say our family has done their part populating Stonewall Crossing."

"Don't be such a grump, Archer. I love how big and happy this family's become. All the laughter and smiles… And, yes, babies. I know you love it, too." Renata smiled.

For the most part, yes. Even if it was a whole lot louder. Three weddings and two sets of twin boys joined the family. He was happy for his brothers—even if he didn't understand the whole falling-in-love, start-a-family thing. They seemed happy; that's all that mattered. "I'll talk to Fisher about the horse."

"Good. Until then, I can ride them?"

He nodded, heading toward the office. "I'm going to change." He was stopped by two different employees, signed off on a delivery and inspected a saddle that needed repair. Once he was in his office, he shrugged out of his still-wet shirt and dropped it on the chair by his desk. A sandwich sat on his desk, a note beside it.

Come to the Lodge for dinner tonight. 7 p.m. Love you—Dad.

He laid the note down and glanced at the clock. It was already four.

The muffled, "Ow, damn it, shit," from Eden's office had him running next door. "Eden?" He stepped inside, but she wasn't sitting at the desk. She was on the floor, rubbing her calf.

"Scorpion," she said, looking up. "And no, it wasn't in my shoe. It just climbed up my leg and bit me."

He tried not to smile as he knelt by her side, lifting her hands. "They're inconsiderate that way." He ran his thumb over the reddened mark. It was the wrong time to notice how soft her skin was. Or soak up just how sweet she smelled this close. He cleared his throat. "I'll get you some ice. And Tylenol." He tried not to stare at her…

Her hazel gaze met his.

He felt immobilized, trapped—in a good way. Other than family, he tended to avoid women. They made him nervous. But not now. Now… He wanted to stay right here, close to her. He didn't know why, exactly, just that being near her was surprisingly… pleasant. It made him feel good. If she wasn't in pain.

"Thank you," she whispered.

He nodded, pushing off the floor. His brain was processing this odd development as he pulled an ice pack from the break room freezer and some pain reliever from the medicine cabinet mounted in his bathroom. By the time he'd returned, he had no reasonable explanation for his reaction to her. He'd barely touched her, but the tips of his fingers and thumb felt like they'd been zapped by 220 volts of electricity. He paused inside her office, studying her as she sat at her desk, staring out the small window.

Her long blond hair fell over her shoulder, loosely braided.

Damn it. He wasn't one to give much thought to such things but...she was beautiful.

He swallowed, beginning to accept that his reaction had no reasonable explanation. Being a man of research, he had to know. "Take these," he said, placing the bottle on the table. He knelt, his fingers encircling her ankle and placing her foot on his leg. Damn, but it was the same. Her scent— He damn near groaned. His gut tightened, his fingers burned and his lungs emptied 'til he ached... He stared at her ankle, stunned.

"I'm fine," she muttered, her voice sounding off—tight and thick.

He looked up at her again, wary. "This will help stop it from swelling." She had no right to be irritated. *He* was the one who'd just been knocked for a loop.

"Okay," she said, sliding her foot from his knee and holding out her hand. "Thank you." She bent, pressing the ice pack to the red welt along her calf.

He stood, his hands on his hips. What the hell was he doing? She was perfectly capable of taking care of herself. She was capable of taking care of an entire family on her own. Family as in a baby and a little girl. A little girl he'd made cry.

"I didn't mean to upset your daughter," he said. "I just… I… She's little."

"I know she's little." Eden looked up at him then. "Contrary to what you think, I would never put my daughter at risk, Dr. Boone. I wasn't planning on letting her touch Fester, but I didn't think it would hurt to get closer to the barn. Fester is not the only horse to see. I wasn't going to let her touch any of them. She's never been around horses. Or cowboys. Your world."

He *was* an asshole. He hadn't just hurt Ivy's

feelings. He'd hurt Eden's, as well—he heard it in her voice. But little girls were outside his comfort zone. Women were outside his comfort zone. And hurt feelings? He didn't have the time or patience for that.

All he knew was Ivy was small. And delicate. Just like Eden. Fester could have hurt them without trying. He swallowed, surprised by the cold, hard fear that stuck in his throat. "It's my business to ensure that the people on the refuge are safe, Miss Caraway... That's all. I did not mean to offend you." He stopped, staring at her. "I apologize."

She blinked, her features softening. "I accept."

He nodded, wishing he knew what she was thinking. His family was full of emotive, unguarded people—he knew where he stood with them. Eden Caraway, however, was an enigma.

Her gaze shifted to her work. "The girls won't come here again—"

That wasn't what he wanted. "Miss Caraway—"

"Unless you, or someone you approve of, is with them," she finished. "I respect your judgment. As we discussed earlier, I am not a horse person."

He nodded again, instantly relieved.

Her eyes bounced from her papers, to him, then back again. The fluid shift of her features catching his full attention. And the red cast of her cheeks. She drew in a deep breath, her gaze holding his. "Dr. Boone—"

"Archer," he corrected, waiting.

"Now that we've reached an understanding..." She paused, her eyes falling from his. "You can go find your...a shirt."

He looked down. He'd heard her and hadn't bothered getting dressed. He didn't say a word as he left her small office and returned to his. He dug through the bag he kept ready for a rescue or house call and tugged on the white undershirt inside. He glanced at his door, still out of sorts, before flopping into his desk chair. This "trying to be on his best behavior" thing wasn't working out.

He ran a hand over his face and glanced at his computer. An email caught his eye.

He slid his reading glasses on and sat forward, poring over the email. Another Boone cousin, from West Texas, had found a horse that needed help and sent the info. The pics Scarlett sent tore at Archer's heart.

This poor little paint horse had been trapped

inside a too-small stall with moldy grain and a bucket of brackish water. No doubt it had intestinal parasites. Possibly lung infection. If it hadn't been moving around, hoof problems…

He spent the next two hours working on the computer, returning phone calls and verifying the location of the horse. Once that was done, he called Deacon.

"I'll head out now," his cousin said. "Be back as soon as I can."

"She's in a bad way," Archer said.

"I'll be careful with her, Archer," Deacon assured him.

"Take Toben," Archer offered. "Don't know how steady she's going to be on her feet."

"Can I take someone I'm less likely to punch?" Deacon asked.

Archer smiled. "You pick. See you later. Don't let Toben drive."

"Not a problem," Deacon agreed.

He placed his phone on the desk, sat back and rubbed a hand over his face.

"Everything okay?" Eden asked from the door.

"New horse coming in." He looked at her. "How's the sting?"

She shrugged. "A little sore. Not so bad."

He nodded.

"Guess juggling scorpion bites and horse rescues and uncooperative employees is all part of a day's work?" she asked, leaning against the door frame.

He couldn't stop the smile. "Yep."

She shook her head, studying him intently. "Have you always wanted to do this? Work with horses, I mean. Be a safe haven for them."

"I knew I'd work with animals. Horses are the animals I understand best, people included." He shrugged. "It was my mom's idea to start the refuge here," he said. "The first horse I ever bought was in bad shape. Abused, mean, mangy. I spent every cent I had to make him my...friend. Took some time, but that horse was my mom's favorite. She and Dad started bringing in strays and letting me work with them. We had a good handler back then, knew horses, how to read them, like the back of his hand. He taught me everything I know. Horses got easier. People not so much." He smiled. "That was it."

She wore a thoughtful expression. "Nice to have such support for your passion. And that your passion became your work."

"Not the same thing?" he asked, curious. "Passion and work?"

"No." She shook her head. "I have a knack for numbers and business. My passion is my girls. And leaving them every morning is a struggle. But it's what I have to do."

He glanced at the clock and stood. "And now you're late getting to them."

"Clara's with them."

"Not the same as having their mother," he said. He knew. Losing his mother had forever changed his life. Partly because the one person in the family who seemed to accept his quirks was gone. She'd prodded him with questions, lured him out on long rides and eased him into sharing his thoughts. She'd always made time for him. It didn't matter how long it had been since his mother's death; the ache was still there, pressing in on him.

"Dr. Boone?"

"Archer," he inserted.

"Archer." She sighed. "I can walk, if you still have work to do."

He shook his head, needing a break. "I'll come back after dinner." He eyed his untouched sandwich, and his stomach growled.

She smiled. And just like that, his tension eased. He wasn't sure he liked the effect Eden Caraway was having on him. But as long as she wasn't too close to him and he wasn't touching her, he seemed to have things under control. She'd be gone soon, and it wouldn't matter. But thoughts of her leaving didn't provide the instant relief he'd expected.

Chapter 5

Eden changed out of her slacks and blouse, slipping into some black leggings and a comfy, light blue tunic. She wanted to be with the girls, enjoy some family time and relax. Something she was completely incapable of around Archer Boone.

Seeing him shirtless had been alarming. It had been years since her body had thrummed with awareness—and want. When he'd knelt at her side, she'd fisted her hands to keep from touching him. The balls of his shoulders, the muscles flexing in his arms and chest. He was gorgeous. More so because he'd earned those muscles through something he was passionate about. When he'd touched her, her senses had gone into overdrive… When his work-roughened fingers had brushed her hands aside to inspect the bite, she'd glimpsed the look in his blue eyes. He seemed concerned. Like he cared.

And she didn't know how she felt about that.

She needed to be more intentional about putting space between them. She'd always been goal-oriented. And her goal had nothing to do with blue eyes and rippling muscles and everything to do with proving herself to her father. This was her chance to grab his attention and his respect. A chance that might not come again.

Lily was rolling on the floor of their room, pushing up onto her knees to rock back and forth.

"You can do it," Eden said, dropping down onto the floor beside her daughter. "Come on. Come get me," she encouraged, holding her hands out.

Lily grinned, rocking with more gusto and falling forward onto her face. Luckily, Eden had placed a quilt on the floor so Lily didn't hurt herself. But she was upset nonetheless. She wailed, turning bright blue eyes on Eden.

"It's okay, sweetie." Eden scooped her up. "It's a lot of work. But you'll get there. Crawling, then walking… And then I'm in real trouble."

"Ma-ma-ma-ma," Lily chanted as soon as she was in her mother's arms, smiling up at Eden.

"I love you so much, little bug." Eden pressed a kiss to each of her daughter's cheeks.

"Momma, Momma," Ivy said in a singsong voice as she came running in. "I made biscuits!"

"You did?" Eden exclaimed. "I love biscuits."

"You have to share," Ivy said. "Clara helped."

"Oh, good." Eden smiled, hugging Ivy close with her other arm. "You're being such a helper, Ivy. Thank you."

Ivy nodded. "'Course, Momma."

"Ba-ba-ba," Lily cooed.

"Did you have fun today?" she asked. "What did you and Clara and Lily do?"

"Mr. Teddy showed us the goats," Ivy said. "Tiny baby ones, too."

Eden smiled. "Baby goats?"

"They make funny sounds. And crawl." Ivy looked at Lily. "Better than Lily."

Lily smiled at Ivy, reaching out to grab Ivy's hand. She adored her big sister.

"What else did you do?" Eden asked.

"Feed them," Ivy said, poking Lily's nose with her pointer finger. Lily giggled, closing her eyes every time Ivy touched her nose.

"What do they eat?" Eden asked, smiling at her girls.

"Corn," Ivy said. "We having corn, too. Come on." She wriggled out of Eden's hold and grabbed her hand. "Come on. Dinner's ready."

"Oh." Eden stood, shifting Lily to her hip, and followed Ivy across the main living room and through a thick wooden door.

Clara was setting the long wooden table while Mr. Boone was placing cups on the place mats.

"Can I help?" Eden asked, struck once more by the crackling dynamic between Teddy Boone and her more-mother-than-nanny.

"No." Clara frowned at her. "You sit and let us take care of you."

Eden counted seven plates. "We're not eating in the dining room?" she asked. "I'd hate to intrude on your family."

Teddy Boone laughed. "No intrusion. It's

mostly me and my daughter, Renata, these days. Archer sometimes, when he remembers to eat. The rest of my sons have wives and kids. Lots of kids."

"But no granddaughters," Clara said, shaking her head.

Eden laughed. "How many?"

Teddy brought a large pitcher of tea to the table. "Let's see. Hunter and Josie have one so far. Fisher and Kylee have two. And Kylee's little brother, Shawn. And Ryder and Annabeth have three. Doc had told Annabeth they were having twins and one was a girl. I can't tell you how relieved Ryder was when they were both boys. Not sure he could handle being daddy to a girl—he used to be quite the ladies' man, you see."

"So you have five children?" Eden asked, bouncing Lily on her knee.

Teddy nodded. "Four boys, one girl. Renata and Fisher are twins. You've met Renata?"

She nodded. "She's very nice."

"She is that." Teddy beamed with pride. "She's her mother made over. Never met a stranger. Never had a mean word to say about a person."

"That doesn't mean I don't think them

every once in a while," Renata Boone said as she entered the kitchen. "Thanks for singing my praises, Dad." She hugged her father and pressed a kiss to his cheek.

Eden watched, moved by the show of love and appreciation between father and daughter. She and her father had been close when she was little. But the last few years Jason Monroe had changed. Now he didn't believe in giving out praise or attention unless it was warranted. And apparently, Eden had yet to earn either. Something she was determined to change. She saw how it was between her father and brother, how easy their relationship was. If she kept trying, kept working, she'd have that, too—she just couldn't give up.

"Who are these two adorable young ladies?" Renata stared down at Ivy. "You are without a doubt the cutest thing I have ever seen."

"Tank you," Ivy said. "You pretty."

"Thank you," Renata answered. "So are you. I'm Renata. Who are you?"

"I'm Ivy."

Renata held her hand out. "Nice to meet you, Ivy. I can tell by looking at you that Eden's your mom. Pretty momma, pretty babies."

Ivy nodded. "And that's Lily, my sister. She can't crawl yet. And she doesn't eat corn."

Renata nodded, looking confused.

"They went to see the baby goats today," Teddy Boone offered as an explanation. "Baby goats crawl on all fours. Like babies."

"Aw, right," Renata said with a smile. "Nope, no corn for Lily yet."

"I think we're ready," Teddy said.

"Smells good," Eden said, sliding Lily into the high chair and snapping on a bib.

"Just grilled some chicken. Corn on the cob. And a salad fresh from the garden." Teddy put the serving platters on the table.

"And biscuits," Ivy said.

"Yes, ma'am, can't forget those. They're the best part," Teddy said, patting Ivy's cheek.

Ivy sat between Clara and Teddy, smiling proudly. Serving dishes were passed, drinks were poured and conversation never stopped. Eden put a few Cheerios on Lily's tray and served herself.

"Sorry I'm late." Archer paused inside the kitchen, his gaze sweeping the room.

"Dr. Boone, I made biscuits," Ivy announced.

Archer smiled. "You did?"

"Clara helped," Ivy added.

"Sounds safe," he said, crossing to the table.

Only one seat was open, the one next to Eden. And when he sat beside her, she nodded at him. Try as she might, she was acutely aware of his presence, his scent and her instant reaction to him.

"Day two," Renata said. "How's it going?"

Had it only been two days? In two days they'd argued; she'd been bitten by a scorpion and adopted by a horse; and she'd questioned her mother's past and her father's motivation; and been offered a permanent position by a man she was far too attracted to. Thank God it was just attraction. It was… Anything more would be oddly out of character. She didn't rush into things. She was careful, methodical. She kept her heart under control.

She put her fork on the table, glancing at Archer.

His attention was fixed on his plate, even as the rest of the table waited for an answer.

She swallowed and said, "Fine." Was it fine? She wasn't feeling very fine at the moment. She was feeling peculiar. She was *not* interested in Archer Boone.

"Fine?" Teddy asked. "Meaning you're feeling better about the budget review, son?"

Eden's heart picked up. He didn't fit in her life. Her goal. And…he was only interested in what she could do for him—like every other man in her life.

"I have every confidence in Miss Caraway's skills." Archer's answer was soft.

She glanced at him.

He looked at her.

She was fully aware that conversation kept going. But she had no idea what the topic of discussion was. Or who was talking. Archer was staring at her, his blue eyes intent and searching. And she was…desperate for air.

"Fester came back," Archer said, his gaze wandering leisurely over her face.

"I'm glad." She was glad. About Fester.

"I'd like you to reconsider my offer," he said.

"What offer?" Teddy Boone asked.

"I want Miss Caraway to consider staying here as the new bookkeeper. And if she's interested, help me with Fester." His attention shifted to the food on his plate.

She couldn't stay. Even setting aside the goal she'd set for herself, it would never work.

First, she was lying about her identity. Once he knew who she really was, any civility would go out the window. Second, there was this *thing* between her and Archer Boone, which made her vulnerable—she didn't like being vulnerable. And finally, this was the sort of place, the sort of family, that would be easy to get tangled up in. She had enough scars on her heart; she didn't want to risk her daughters, too.

"While I appreciate the offer, I know I'm not the right person for the job," she answered. "Your biscuits are yummy, Ivy. Good job."

"Fester might disagree," Archer pressed.

"Fester is a horse," she said, glancing at him.

"Fine, *I* disagree," he continued.

"That's unfortunate." She put more cereal on Lily's tray. "And that was a polite attempt to change the conversation."

Archer sat back, crossed his arms over his chest and scowled at her. And she pointedly ignored him.

Teddy Boone chuckled.

"Where are you off to next?" Renata asked. "Do temps normally travel for jobs?"

Since she had no idea, she shrugged. She knew Clara was uncomfortable with her little deception, so she'd answer as honestly as she could. "Normally I'm in Houston. But occasionally I've been sent out for special reviews or audits." Which was true.

"You like Houston?" Teddy asked. "I've been a few times, for stock shows and auctions, and the occasional rodeo. Big city. Lots of traffic. Nice people, for the most part."

She'd never thought about it. It was where her family was. Yes, she'd thought about leaving after her mother's death, but she knew her father would consider that a betrayal. And once you got on his bad side, there was no going back. "It's home."

"What about your husband?" Renata asked. "He's got to be missing his ladies."

"Dad's on a trip," Ivy offered. "'Mergency."

"An emergency?" Renata repeated. "I hope everything's okay?"

"Clark travels extensively for work," Eden said. "This was his week with the girls, but something came up." She smiled at Lily, her baby girl's grin filling her heart with love. She was glad something had come up. Life was better, even in a state of chaos, with her daughters close.

"Got to meet goats," Ivy said. "And make biscuits."

"And they're good," Teddy Boone said. "Real good."

"Tank you." Ivy bounced in her seat. "I don't cook at Daddy's house. But I cook at Momma's. She doesn't mind messes. And she lets me lick the spoon."

Archer was staring at her, she could feel it. Would she see disappointment or curiosity? Did it matter? She spooned more applesauce and oatmeal into Lily's mouth. Lily promptly spit half back out. Before grinning.

"Are you done?" she asked Lily.

Lily slapped her hands on the tray, cooing.

"I am sorry, Eden," Renata said. "Your personal life is none of my business. Lily's so young I assumed—"

"It's fine." Eden smiled at Renata.

Most people didn't divorce mid-pregnancy. Clark had wanted to wait, said he'd try harder—he'd be faithful this time. But Eden knew better. Clark didn't have monogamy in his DNA. And Eden couldn't stomach continuing to turn a blind eye to his constant indiscretions. They'd gone to counseling, taken a romantic vacation—Lily was the result—but they'd been back a month before Clark went back to his old ways. He couldn't keep it in his pants. She'd petitioned for a divorce when she was fifteen weeks pregnant, against the advice of her father.

Clark didn't fight it. But her father made the whole ordeal a nightmare. If he could choose, Eden had no doubt her father would pick Clark over Eden. In a way he had—giving Clark a promotion at the firm while Eden was moved off the main floor into the Audit and Review office.

Lily rubbed her eyes, smearing applesauce and oatmeal into the golden curls atop her little head. "I think it's bath and bedtime for Lily. If you'll excuse me."

"I'll keep your food warm," Clara offered.

"Thank you. Finish up, Ivy, almost bath time," Eden said.

"Okay, Momma." Ivy nodded. "Night, Lily."

Lily smiled at Ivy, her little legs kicking as Eden held her close and carried her from the kitchen. She kissed her baby girl's temple as they crossed the great room and headed to their suite, loving Lily's weight in her arms, her sweet baby smell a comfort.

"Ma-ma-ma-ma," Lily said, tugging a fistful of Eden's hair.

"That's me," Eden agreed, gently removing her hair from Lily's hold. "I'm your momma, little bug." She kissed her daughter's temple, thinking about the kiss Renata Boone had given her own father.

She hadn't wanted to get personal. She didn't want to talk about Clark or her family. These were good people. And she was deceiving them. Something she'd never planned on doing. Something that was growing increasingly difficult to do.

Having dinner with the Boones was no longer an option. Or spending time with the family, beyond what was required for work. Her stomach felt leaden.

If only she could forget what Renata had said that first night. If she could forget that her mother was directly involved with the refuge, maybe she wouldn't feel as conflicted as she was beginning to feel. And yet, she worried about what she might find out. Her mother hadn't been happy in her marriage… She thought about Teddy Boone. The man was everything her father wasn't. Warm, kind and handsome. Had her mother been unfaithful? And could Eden live with that? She knew how degrading it felt to be the one cheated on.

Maybe there were some things best left alone. Things like second-guessing her goals. And Archer Boone. Definitely Archer Boone.

She needed to focus and finish up so she could leave—before things got complicated.

She pressed a kiss to Lily's forehead and gathered supplies for bath. "Bath time, Lily." Lily grinned, all dimples, blond curls and wide eyes. "Ba-la-ma-ba-ba."

Eden giggled, wondering how Ivy would translate that one. No more focusing on things that didn't matter. Her job, her girls—that was enough; it had to be.

Archer held a pink crayon out to Ivy.

"Tank you," she said.

Archer watched her color like mad, not bothering to point out she was coloring outside the lines. She was three. And she was enjoying herself. That, to Archer's mind, was enough.

"Baby goats are loud," she said, not bothering to stop coloring. "Are horses loud, too?"

"They can be," he said, trading her pink for a green.

"Horses are bigger," Ivy said, looking at him. "Giants."

Compared to a goat, yes. He nodded.

"Momma said the big black horse is sad." She started coloring again.

The black horse? Fester? Eden had told Ivy about Fester? He smiled. "Why is he sad?"

"Momma says he's scared of being alone." Ivy sat back, inspecting her coloring book. "Pupple, please?"

He was scared of being alone… "Pupple?" he repeated, putting on his reading glasses to read the name colors on the crayon wrappers.

Ivy reached over him for a crayon. "Pupple," she said.

He smiled, nodding. "Purple."

She went back to coloring her flowers.

"All done, Miss Ivy?" Clara said. "How about I give you your bath so your momma can eat."

"Okay," Ivy said. "Put up my colors first."

Archer held the box while she shoved all of her crayons inside.

"Night, Dr. Boone," she said, smiling at him.

He had no choice but to smile back. "Call me Archer, Miss Ivy."

"Night, Dr. Archer," she said before running to Clara.

Clara scooped her up and carried her down the hall.

"It's killing you not to organize them, isn't it?" Renata asked.

"What?" He turned to find his sister perched on the arm of his chair, watching him closely.

"The crayons. All the colors mixed up like that. Your OCD has to be going crazy," she teased. "You can sort them. I won't judge you."

He arched a brow at her.

"Okay, maybe a little judging." Renata giggled. "You're right about the blue mare. Sweetest ride ever. You've got to name her, by the way."

"Her owner should name her," Archer said.

"If Shawn doesn't take her, I'd like to," Renata said, moving to the chair across from him.

"Okay."

"What's up with Dad?" she asked.

"What do you mean?"

She shook her head, rolling her eyes. "Nothing. I love you, big brother, but your cluelessness never fails to amaze me."

He frowned. "What are you talking about?"

"Dad's all chipper," she said, waiting.

"He's always chipper," he countered. "It's damn annoying at five in the morning."

Renata laughed.

Eden came into the room then. She walked

straight through to the kitchen, nodding in acknowledgment as she passed. Archer watched, trying to think of something to say. But she disappeared behind the door and the moment was lost.

"What do you make of Miss Caraway?" Renata asked.

Archer shot her a look. He sighed. "Why do I feel like this is a loaded question?"

She smiled. "I'm just wondering how far the cluelessness extends."

"Fine, clue me in. I'll be happy to clear up any of your misconceptions."

She sat back. "You like her. Enough to keep her around. And the fact that Fester likes her is driving you nuts—especially since she won't jump on board with your plan."

He didn't say anything. Because there was nothing to correct.

His sister smiled. "What are you going to do?"

"Do?"

Renata shook her head again. "Archer, come on. Out of all my brothers, you are the most tenacious. You make things happen, change people's minds, bring them around, get them excited. You talk people out of money. You—

the surly one. When you want something, you are unstoppable."

"This applies to Miss Caraway how?" He waited. He knew exactly what his sister was saying, but there was no way he was going to admit that his interest in Eden extended outside of work. Playing the obtuse card was his only option.

"What are we talking about?" Their father joined them.

"Where's Eden?" Renata asked.

"She got a phone call so I thought she'd appreciate some privacy." His father slid into his favorite leather recliner. "What are you two worked up over?"

Archer shot him a look.

"Fine, what's Renata worked up over?" Teddy laughed.

"Eden," Renata said, lowering her voice.

"Good momma, that one." Teddy frowned. "That little lady has had more than her fair share of heartache."

Archer stared at his father. "Why do you say that?"

His father looked uncomfortable, shifting in his seat before he answered, "Hell, son, she's been through a divorce already. Her babies are still babies. You don't throw in the towel unless something went seriously wrong. Not in my book, anyway. And she doesn't strike me as the sort to do something without thinking it through." He shrugged. "I caught some of her phone call… I'd say Miss Caraway's life isn't an easy one."

Archer ran a hand over his face. He'd been so caught up in what Fester needed, what he wanted, that he hadn't bothered to consider all of Eden's circumstances. One more reminder that he was a self-absorbed ass. She'd had a long day. And he'd made it longer. Plus the scorpion. And his reprimand. He stood and headed into the kitchen. Eden sat at the table, her elbows resting on the polished wood surface, her chin resting on her palms.

"You okay?" he asked, sitting across from her.

She jumped, immediately wiping her face with her hands. Wiping away tears.

"Eden?" he asked, offering her the handkerchief he always kept in his pocket.

She took it, her murmured thank-you twisting his gut. He sat there, wishing she'd look at him—hoping he could gain some sort of insight into this woman. "Ivy likes purple. She colored all her flowers purple."

Eden smiled. "It's her favorite."

"She asked if horses were as noisy as goats," he continued.

She glanced at him, poking the chicken on her plate with her fork. "What did you tell her?"

"Sometimes." He shrugged. "Maybe she should come down to the barn tomorrow? Meet one up close?"

She laid her fork down and crossed her arms. "Why?"

Her tone was a warning. He needed to be very careful how he responded to her. "She'd like it."

She stood, carrying her still-full plate to the counter. "So it's for Ivy?"

He followed her to the sink, watching her scrape the food into the trash. "Yes."

"Not me?" She slammed the plate on the counter. "You're not trying to get to me through my daughter? So I'll stay and help you with Fester?"

He paused, frowning. "No, Eden. That... wasn't my intent."

Her hazel gaze searched his, brimming with more tears.

His chest felt heavy. He had two choices. Pulling her close, holding her against him, which wasn't something he was comfortable with. Or trying to break the tension, tease her, even if he didn't have the best record with that, either. "I might have tried it—if I thought it would work."

Her eyes widened before she burst out laughing.

He smiled.

She shook her head.

"You didn't eat much," he said.

"Not hungry," she answered, still looking at him.

And the way she was looking at him… He placed his hand on the counter, close to hers. Almost touching her. He wanted to, though. Damn it. He wanted to touch her. He wanted to chase away her sadness. Make her smile. Because her smile was powerful.

"You ever go horseback riding?" he asked.

She nodded. "When I was young."

Which surprised him.

"My mother loved horses. She grew up around them." She broke off suddenly.

My mother loved horses. Past tense. They had that in common. "How about I take you and Ivy for a ride tomorrow?"

She frowned and turned away to wash her plate in the sink. "I don't think that's a good idea," she murmured. "I have too much work to do. And I think it's best if my family eats with the other guests from now on, in the main dining room. I am, after all, an employee. Not family."

Archer stared down at her. "If that's what you'd prefer."

"It is, Dr. Boone." She nodded. "But I appreciate your family's hospitality."

She was doing the right thing, putting up boundaries and distance. But he'd enjoyed having her at the table tonight. Sitting beside her, watching her with Lily, and Ivy's sunny laugh and chatter felt right. And damn good. "Eden, Renata shouldn't have pried—"

Eden shook her head, her hazel eyes locking with his. "I pride myself on being a professional, Dr. Boone. That is what we are. Professionals. Working together for a common goal. I'll see you in the morning."

She left him standing in the kitchen, his sister's words replaying.

When you want something, you are unstoppable.

Did he want Eden? He swallowed, leaning back against the kitchen counter. Yes. He did. In a way that was neither professional nor rational. A realization he was still struggling with. He'd known her only a few days, for crying out loud. What he was considering was rash and careless. He was neither.

But…in a few more days she'd be gone. And if the sense of panic that fact caused was any indication, he needed to decide just what he was going to do about Eden Caraway.

Chapter 6

"Mr. Boone says there will be a parade and pony rides and a carnival on Monday." Clara was braiding Ivy's long ringlets.

"I have to work, Clara." Eden sighed. "I have to get Dr. Boone's finances in order and the board presentation in order by next Friday."

"Pony rides, Momma," Ivy said. "Real ponies."

"I'll ask Dr. Boone. Considering it'll be our last day here, I'm not very optimistic." She hoped working through the weekend would allow her to finish the spreadsheets and scanning. And help her find something useful. In the time she'd been here, she had yet to find a single suspicious purchase or expense. Archer's filing system, or lack thereof, was the only flaw. What she had learned had only increased her respect for Archer Boone and the work he did. The refuge was self-sustaining at this level. They sold horses, held clinics and riding camps, and participated in a large annual fund-raiser. Riders and horse lovers from all over came to participate in an annual scavenger hunt on the several thousand acres that made up Boone Ranch.

Archer wanted to expand the refuge, but his request was modest. A large therapy pool, a more updated barn, a bunkhouse for expanded overnight camps and three new exercise walking wheels. To Eden, it was more maintenance than expansion.

"Ask him, pretty please, Momma," Ivy said, crawling across the bed.

"I'll ask him," Eden promised, kissing her nose. "Silly goose."

Ivy smiled.

"What are you going to do today?" she asked Clara.

"Mr. Boone said he'd take us into town. There's a dollhouse museum and an old-fashioned soda shop." Clara smiled, picking up Lily.

Eden sighed. "You're spending a lot of time with Mr. Boone."

Clara's cheeks colored prettily. "He's being a good ambassador, that's all."

Eden smiled. "Sure. Have fun exploring the town." She kissed them all goodbye and walked out the back door. The path to the refuge was easy enough to follow, and this early, it wasn't miserably hot. She enjoyed the sounds of the birds in the cedar and oak trees. She'd spotted a raccoon, squirrels, a roadrunner and several jackrabbits on her way.

But whatever was following her this morning was larger.

She heard him before she saw him, his soft whinny making her wait. "Fester," she said, stopping so the horse could come closer. "Good morning. Were you waiting for me?" She stood still, letting the animal give her a hug. "You need a brushing." She ran her fingers through his mane on the side of his neck, noting the burs and twigs trapped in the long black hair.

Fester shook his head, making her laugh.

"No brushing?" she asked. "A bath, maybe?" She started walking again, talking to Fester the whole time. He listened, she could tell. His ears cocked toward her, the occasional nicker a sort of conversation.

By the time they reached the refuge, Eden slowed, placing her hand on the horse's neck. She paused by the steps of the administration office. "I wish you could tell me what you wanted, Fester. Archer wants to make you happy. So do I." She rubbed his well-muscled neck with long, slow strokes.

"That's all he wants," Archer said, his voice low and coaxing.

Fester's ears twitched, but he stayed by her side.

"What?" Eden asked.

"You," Archer said. "I've never seen him so calm."

She glanced at Archer, painfully aware of how handsome he looked in his pressed button-down shirt and tight, worn jeans. She continued stroking Fester's neck, smiling when Fester turned toward her, breathing against her chest. "He's a beautiful boy." She saw the heavy scarring along his back right leg. "What happened to him?"

"He was caught in barbed wire when I got the call. Half-starved and dehydrated, trapped and pissed at the world. His leg was in a bad way. Think he blames me for the pain he went through." Archer moved a little closer, keeping his voice low.

"It's easy to lash out, isn't it?" she asked Fester. "But Archer's a friend. Where were his owners?"

"A couple owned him pretty much his whole life. The husband got sick so they moved up north to their daughter's place. They thought someone had come to get him, but…"

"He was left behind." She rested her forehead against Fester's neck and closed her eyes, overcome with sympathy for the animal. Fester didn't know where his people went. All he knew was he was alone. He must have been terrified, waiting for his people, trapped and hurting. "Does he like other horses?" she asked.

Archer sat on the bottom step of the porch, a few feet away.

Fester made an odd sound, stepping back.

"Don't know. He gets agitated and jumps the fence as soon as the gate closes—before he sees the other horses." Archer shook his head.

Eden stared at the horse. "Can we try again?"

Archer didn't answer right away. "We can.

He needs everyone to know he's in charge. He's special."

Eden looked at Archer, hesitant. "Is there a group that won't challenge him? Timid animals? That might want a leader?"

"We could try to get him in with the two waiting to be companion animals," Toben called out from where he was leaning on the porch railing, keeping his distance but close enough to hear. "Can't get more docile than that."

"Bring them up to the front pasture, so we can break them up if we need to," Archer said, standing.

"On it," Toben said, sprinting off.

"Question is, how do we convince him to go inside a gate?" Archer sighed.

She already knew the answer to that. She rested her hand on the horse's back. "I'll walk in with him. Stay for a while."

"Eden, I don't want you trapped inside. If he does get riled up—"

"You'll tell me before that happens. You're the animal behaviorist. Would Fester hurt me?" Her gaze locked with his.

There was a long pause, his blue eyes boring into her own. "No, he loves you." His voice was low, gruff.

It was hard to breathe. "Why do you say that?"

"He stays close to you. When he sees you, he comes. Hell, he's putting himself between you and me right now—protecting you." Archer ran a hand over his face. "If you figure out a way to make me a good guy, let me know."

Eden heard the anguish in his voice and hurt for him. This was Archer's life. He wanted to help the stubborn, beautiful animal. "I will," she said, meaning it.

Archer's gaze returned to hers. "You don't have to do this."

She nodded, continuing to run her hands along Fester's shoulder. "I do." The longer he stared at her, the heavier her chest felt. She didn't know what he was thinking, but she knew exactly how she was responding. If he took one step toward her, she'd close the gap.

"We're ready," Toben called out.

Eden tore her gaze from Archer's and walked toward the gate Toben had opened. Fester nickered at her, so she stopped and waited for him to catch up.

The whole refuge seemed to be waiting. Eden had never felt it so still. Maybe that's why Fester seemed nervous. His ears were

rotating wildly and his tail swished erratically. He didn't like the pressure, either. She
kept walking, talking to him in a soft, reas-
suring voice.

Eventually he followed her, hesitating just
inside the gate. She kept going, crossing between the two horses in the pasture to rest
against the wooden fence post. "Come on,
Fester. You need some friends," she called
out. "Come on."

Fester whinnied. The other two horses'
ears perked up. One whinnied in answer.

Eden stood there, terrified and hopeful. It
took forever before Fester followed her into
the pasture. When he did, he ignored the
other horses and stood off to the side, looking at her. She kept on talking while the other
horses approached.

"He's making them come to him." Archer's
voice was at her ear. "That's good. Lets them
know he's in charge. Neither of them will
challenge that."

"What happens now?" she asked.

"We wait," Archer said.

Archer spent the next minutes explaining
the animals' posturing, the noises they made,
the slow easing of Fester's tension. When
Fester made his way to the water trough,

the other two slowly followed, staying close to him.

Eden smiled. "That's good, right?" She looked at Archer, full of hope.

He was smiling, too, watching the horses. "Yes, ma'am. It's good."

She'd like to think the rapid thump of her heart was due to Fester's newfound herd. But the strong profile, the full lips and the fine crinkles at the corner of Archer's smiling eyes were the more likely cause.

His blue gaze shifted to her, his smile dazzling.

The longer she stood there, staring at him, the harder it was to look away. But she managed it, barely. "Ivy heard about the parade. On Monday?"

"Stonewall Crossing knows how to throw a parade. You're not heading back to Houston until the middle of next week, are you?" His question was gruff.

"I planned on working through the weekend."

He shook his head. "We'll get it done without giving up your weekend. Your girls are here, Eden. As long as we get it done by the end of next week, we should be fine."

End of next week? She'd assumed, since

Archer was so gung ho to get everything done, weekends wouldn't matter. She'd counted on leaving with plenty of time to prepare for the board meeting on Friday—not that she had anything to present to the board. Why was that such a relief? "Our tickets are booked for early Tuesday morning."

His smile dimmed. "That'd be a shame, Eden. Stay, for the parade and the fireworks, too," he said. "I'm happy to cover the cost of your ticket change, fly you home Thursday morning. That'll give us plenty of time."

Us. She shouldn't like the sound of that. But she did. She frowned. Another reason to leave—as soon as possible.

Fester went trotting by, his two new companions in tow. Fester's confidence and posturing was a thing of beauty. He was enjoying the company, and it made her happy, too happy. She shouldn't be this happy over a horse. She swallowed, pushing off the fence. "Think it's okay for me to get to work now?" she asked, avoiding eye contact.

He stepped back. "Guess we'll find out." He held his hand out, offering to help her slide between the fence slats. But Eden did it on her own, made sure Fester was still happy and hurried inside.

* * *

Archer was disappointed. Seeing Fester coming into his own, being receptive to the enclosed arena, was a breakthrough. Yet news of Eden's plans, her apparent eagerness to leave, gnawed at him. And it lingered, a bruise deep beneath the skin.

Why, he didn't know. She'd made it clear she had no interest in staying here. She'd been nothing but honest with him, never waffled or offered him any false hope. Once she was done with his books, she would leave him—leave here.

What he wanted, what he may or may not be feeling, wouldn't change that.

When he greeted his cousin Deacon later that afternoon he was still growling. The sight of Deacon's beat-up horse trailer and an ancient Chevy pickup truck did little to lift his spirits. In fact, the music blaring from Deacon's open windows only ratcheted up his irritation.

"Archer," Deacon said, nodding and turning down the music—a little. "Brought you a little something. And by little, I mean she'd be knocked down by a strong breeze. She's weak on her feet. You're gonna need some manpower to get her out."

Archer nodded. "Bring her around to the end of the small barn," he asked. "Got some of the men waiting to help unload."

Deacon nodded, pulling slowly forward.

Archer caught a glimpse of the skeletal animal with sad eyes and shook his head. At least she was here. She had a fighting chance now.

It had been one hell of a long day. Fester was behaving, but Archer had asked Renata to keep a close eye on him—at least during his shift at the vet hospital. He'd made his rounds quickly, pleased that his students were finally getting the knack of charting. He knew he was tough on them, but there was no room for error.

He'd had to step in to lecture a class since his brother Hunter had called in sick—something his big brother never did. After he was done at the hospital, he'd stopped by the lumberyard for the fencing materials his father had requested and the feed store, too. He'd arrived at the refuge to see Eden watching Fester from the front porch, all smiles. She'd seen him climb out of his truck and scurried inside without a backward glance.

If Deacon hadn't been bringing in the new horse, he'd have taken River on a long ride.

He needed to clear his head—think of things beyond the Monroe Foundation and Eden Caraway.

"Got plans?" Toben asked Deacon. "Dancing at Cutter's place tonight."

Archer didn't answer; he knew Toben wasn't asking him. He opened the larger stall the horse would start out in. It was open at the end, giving her a view of the outside—where she'd be free to run when she'd regained some of her strength.

Deacon shrugged. "Drove most of last night. My plans were food and bed."

"Damn shame, Deacon," Toben said. "Whole family's coming, according to Hunter. Uncle Teddy's even bringing a date."

That grabbed Archer's attention. Hunter? He'd called in sick to work but could go out dancing? And his father? On a date?

"Might have to have a beer, then." Deacon relented, then emphasized, "One."

Archer didn't say a thing. His father had one love in his life. And when Archer's mother died, that part of his dad's heart had stopped working. While his siblings worried over him, Archer understood. If you loved someone that completely, how would you get over losing them? Not that Archer had any

experience with love—beyond his family.
Maybe it was seeing his father's heart so utterly destroyed. Or the countless girls his own
brother Ryder wounded in his youth. Whatever it was, Archer had kept women and romance and hearts and flowers at arm's length.

No way his father was dating. Archer
shook his head but held his tongue. Nope. He
didn't believe it. Instead of letting his cousins' chatter distract him, he concentrated on
what needed to be done: settling this horse.

She was in bad shape. Shaking and blowing hard after a few steps.

"The shed she was in was dark and damn
dirty," Deacon offered. "I'm thinking she ran
there for cover and the roof caved in."

Archer nodded, seeing how resistant she
was to leaving the dim trailer. He stepped
inside, offering his hands and speaking to
the skittish horse in low tones. She was so
little, so frail, her skin jumping and twitching out of pure agitation. Her ears cocked up,
but she looked side to side, disoriented and
frightened.

He took his time, inspecting the horse from
nose to tail. A small paint horse, black and
white. One blue eye, one brown. Filmy eyes.
Could be from malnutrition, could be cata-

racts. Either way, it would add to the horse's agitation. New place. Blurred vision.

He placed a light hand on the horse's back, the skin flinching beneath his touch. He could feel the notches of the animal's spine, the line of each rib.

"You're okay," he said. "We'll keep you safe."

"She blind?" Deacon asked.

"Might be." Archer kept his hand on the horse. She leaned into him, nudging his head, knocking his hat to the ground. "Don't like my hat?" He laughed softly.

Deacon nodded. "She's got more spirit than I expected."

"Which is good. Long road to recovery. Need to do some blood work, check for parasites, vitamin deficiencies…" Archer kept a soothing tone, aware of every twitch and turn, shift and whiffle the horse made. She needed quiet, to feel calm and safe. Archer respected that—and took care to make sure the little paint understood he meant no harm. "We're going to need help getting her out. She's favoring her front left hoof. Don't want to stress her out."

It took forty-five minutes and six men to get the horse into the stall and settled. He spent another hour watching her, making notes on her gait, her wheeze, the constant shaking of her head. He wrote out a detailed diet plan and a series of vaccinations and medicines that would help get her back on her feet.

He nodded goodbye to Toben, thanked Deacon for the delivery and sat against the stall fence. He was in no hurry. After a while, she approached him, sniffing him curiously, growing accustomed to him. He suspected she'd be with him for a long time. Sometimes a horse stayed. They were too broken or too fragile to move again. "You're okay, little girl," he murmured. "Rest easy now."

"Dr. Boone?" Eden's voice was soft.

The horse's ears pricked forward, turning toward her.

"In here. Calm, soothing tones, please," he said, staying put.

"Oh." Her exclamation was confirmation she'd found him.

"What can I do for you?" he asked, catching sight of her at the fence. Her golden hair was slipping free from her bun. She looked tired. And sad. Her hazel eyes inspected the horse, then pressed tightly shut.

"I… I wanted to let you know I was walking back to the Lodge," she murmured.

"You're under no obligation to check in with me," he answered, trying to keep his irritation from seeping into his tone.

But she hesitated.

His teeth ground together, but he didn't say anything.

"Dr. Boone?" she asked.

"Yes, Miss Caraway." The horse stiffened at his tone.

"I respect what you do. And whether or not I'm doing everything you want me to do, I am doing the job I was hired to do." Her tone remained soft. "Even if you're disappointed."

He stood slowly, his gaze slamming into hers over the back of the horse. "You are." He placed a hand on the horse's shoulders. She was right. And he was being...irrational. "I... I appreciate your hard work. And what you did for Fester today, as well." He stopped himself from saying anything else.

Her gaze moved to his hand on the horse's back. "She's in a bad way?"

He nodded.

"Will you stay with her?" she asked, resting her arms on the top of the metal gate leading into the large stall.

He nodded, watching her, wishing she'd stay. This was his job, his area of expertise.

Not hers. But…he liked having her close. Besides, her girls would be missing her.

"What's her name?" she asked, smiling as the horse rubbed Archer's chest with her nose.

"No name," he answered.

Her gaze returned to his. "No name?"

He smiled. "You have a suggestion?"

She shook her head. "I don't know her."

"Exactly," he agreed. "Not yet."

She smiled back. "Oh."

Her smile caught him unaware. Something about it, the softening of her features and the sparkle in her eyes, took a firm hold of him. Not him. But his chest. Deep inside his chest. An ache. And that damn tightening in his throat.

"Well, Clara's having a night out." She stepped back from the gate. "It'll be me and the girls. Lots of purple crayons."

A night with her and her daughters. A night of laughter and hugging and coloring and silliness. And Eden smiling. "Sounds nice," he said.

She laughed then, glancing over her shoulder as she walked out of the barn.

Archer stood there, rigid, hoping that—now that she was gone—he'd feel differently.

Instead, the ache grew. And he began to accept that Eden Caraway had done something he'd thought was impossible. She'd taken a firm grip on his heart. And more surprisingly, Archer didn't mind.

Chapter 7

Archer stalked into the Lodge, tired and irritated. The temporary fix he and his brothers had rigged for his plumbing was no longer working. No water meant no water. And he needed a shower and something to eat before he fell face-first in his bed.

He'd made sure the horse was bedded down, putting his dad's even-keeled mare in the stall next to her. The little paint perked up, exchanging a series of whickers and clicks through the wall. Archer had lingered, but he was dead on his feet. He had Luke, one of the resident hands, bunk down close by with strict orders to call him if anything changed.

He slipped through the back door, knowing it was well after midnight. Most of the guests would be asleep or in town dancing at Cutter's.

He was almost across the great room of the Lodge to his father's small apartment when he saw Eden walking the floor. And damn if seeing her didn't remind him just how much trouble he was in. He'd never cared much how a woman's hair looked, or how graceful she could be dancing back and forth on bare feet. But Eden's hair, almost white in the dim light, captivated him. She swayed in time to the song she was humming softly—so softly he barely heard her. Baby Lily fussed, clearly fighting sleep and losing the battle.

Ivy was sound asleep in the recliner, hugging a large stuffed animal.

From the looks of it, Eden's girls' night wasn't wrapping up so smoothly.

He was crossing the room before he had time to think through what he was doing.

She saw him, her expression almost apologetic.

"Need help?" he whispered.

She kept bouncing Lily. "No, thank you."

"What about Ivy?" he asked, glancing at the sleeping girl. "I can put her to bed."

She smiled, nodding reluctantly.

"Okay?" he asked.

"Please," she murmured, returning to her lullaby.

Archer scooped Ivy up, her weight slight, and her damp hair, fresh from her bath, had an oddly pleasing scent. She curled against his chest, her hiccup-sigh making him smile.

He followed Eden into their suite, neat stacks of puzzles, books and toys lining the walls. And a pile of papers on one bed. Eden had been working. A rhythmic beep sounded. A phone. Her cell phone—lying on the floor across the room. Half hidden by the chair.

He placed Ivy in the trundle bed, covering her with the sheets and blanket. She barely stirred.

When he stepped back, Eden was laying Lily in her crib. She stayed there, staring down at the baby with so much love he ached. She sighed, picking up the phone from the floor and turning it off. She opened a drawer, buried the phone in clothes and shut it with a surprising amount of force.

They both froze, waiting. Neither girl woke.

Her shoulders drooped. In defeat? Or exhaustion? Not that it was any of his business.

And that's when he realized he was standing in her bedroom. He was intruding. This was her world, a world of sleepless nights, complications, sticky fingers and compromise. A world he didn't want—a world he hadn't been invited into. No matter how this woman made him feel, he'd be a fool to want any of this.

He slipped from the room, staring out the large floor-to-ceiling windows that lined the back of the Lodge. The view was incredible. On a clear night like tonight, the ranch seemed endless—edging the horizon. This was his world.

"Thank you," she said, making him jump.

He glanced at her, his nerves on edge. It didn't help that she was in a nightgown, not a suit or slacks. And her hair was down, not in a braid or bun. That odd tightening clamped around his throat, making it damn challenging to breathe. He had no right to ask, but he did, anyway. "Everything all right?"

She wrapped her arms around her waist, the hitch in her breath hard to miss. "Have you ever felt trapped, Archer?"

He looked at her then. "No." Her answering smile was sad. And it made that ache in his chest unbearable. "Are you trapped, Eden?"

She shook her head.

He waited, the slight space between them crackling with something he'd never experienced before.

She looked at him then. "I guess I am."

He turned toward her, shoving his hands into his pockets so he wouldn't do something stupid. "How?"

She hesitated. "My dad. My ex-husband. I can't seem to do anything right. It's…defeating."

"If they don't respect you, why do you care what they think?" He ached to comfort her.

"It's that easy?" she asked.

He nodded. "If it's not, it should be."

She smiled, shaking her head. "Well. I work for my father. And my ex-husband works for him, as well."

Archer frowned. "You're kidding me. Why?"

"Which?" she asked. "Why do I work for my father? Or why does my ex work for my father?"

He nodded, trying to understand her predicament. "Both."

"It's complicated," she said, clearly uncomfortable. "I have responsibilities." She glanced at the open door to her suite.

He watched her, noting the crease that

formed between her brows and the way her mouth pulled down at the corners. "Uncomplicate it. Work for me. I'm an asshole. You know it. But I'd make sure you could care for your family."

She looked at him. "You're not. Trust me. I know what an asshole is. How words can cut you to ribbons and steal your confidence."

Her sadness infuriated him. "That's not right, Eden."

She shrugged, but he saw the helplessness she was scrambling to hide.

He couldn't take it. How his hands ended up on her shoulders, pulling her close, he didn't know. But the feel of her, soft in his arms, seemed to wipe reason from his brain. He should let her go. He should show her how professional he was, how sincere he was about helping her. Instead of touching her cheek and tipping her face back. Not to kiss her, but to see her. To study her. The curve of her face and huge eyes… He swallowed, stunned and reeling and not sure what the hell was happening.

But she was moving into him, closer. Her hand rested lightly on his chest as she reached up on tiptoe…and kissed him.

Her lips—warm, soft, sweet—pressed

against his. His bones seemed to melt, bonding them together. Her breath wafted across his cheek, her scent filling his nostrils, his lungs. He needed more. All of her, desperately. His fingers slid through the silk of her hair as her hands gripped his shirtfront. His lips parted hers, the heat of her mouth stirring his body to life. Damn but the touch of her tongue on his… He moaned, deep in his throat.

She swayed against him, her breath catching as she clung to him. Too tempting, too yielding. Too perfect.

All that mattered was this: kissing her, tangling his hands in her hair, holding her close, feeling her pressed tight against him. Any thoughts of control and space and danger were replaced by want—need. The slide of her arms twining around his neck, her hands gripping his head, her mouth moving frantically with his. He'd do whatever he had to do to keep her right where she was…

But the front door opened and he heard his father's rumble of a laugh.

Eden was gone, the door to her suite closing before he'd time to recognize she was no longer in his grasp.

"I had a good time," a woman said. "I

haven't danced like that in years. And congratulations on the good news."

"I confess I suspected that's what tonight was about. Hunter and Josie have been trying to have a baby for a while, so this is good news," his father said.

Hunter and Josie were expecting? Archer smiled, happy for his big brother.

"I'm mighty glad you went with me, Clara. I mean it. Now we just need to figure out how to get Eden to stay for a little while longer."

His father. And Clara.

"We do?" Clara's voice.

"I think this place is good for her. And... I'd like to spend more time with you," his father said. "If you're agreeable to the idea?"

There was a slight pause. Archer held his breath, waiting.

"I am." Clara sounded nervous, giddy.

His father *was* dating. That would take some getting used to.

So would accepting that he was falling in love. Especially since he wasn't sure he believed love really existed.

Eden smiled as Ivy chattered away about the shape of her pancakes, how many strawberries she was going to eat and that she preferred the long sausages to the round flat ones. Eden was too tired to eat. Instead she downed cups of coffee, hating the nervous knot sitting hard and heavy in her stomach.

What had she done?

During their divorce, Clark had used a slew of unflattering, unfeeling adjectives to justify his wandering eye. Words like *cold*, *aloof*, *frigid* and *distant*. The ice queen.

Not the sort of woman who would kiss a man in her nightgown. Kiss and kiss until her body was on fire. The want Archer Boone unleashed was unexpected. Powerful. Raw. She sucked in a deep breath, placing her coffee cup on the table with a thud.

It was a mistake. One she needed to learn from. Now she knew how dangerous he was—just how intense their attraction was. And kissing him? She couldn't let it happen again.

Clara glanced at her, so she smiled at Lily, stroked Ivy's cheek and tried to engage.

"No teeth," Ivy was saying. "So they peck."

"Chickens," Clara offered.

Eden nodded. "Thank you."

"Peck peck peck," Ivy said, eyeing the crumbs on her plate.

"But little girls have teeth." Eden smiled.

"And hands and fingers to help feed themselves."

Ivy grinned sweetly. "'Course, Momma."

Eden laughed. "And what do they eat?"

"Corn," Ivy said. "And cake crumbs. And cookies. And pie crumbs."

Eden and Clara exchanged a knowing look.

"Lucky chickens," Eden said, sipping her coffee.

Ivy nodded. "I want one."

"I'm not sure they'd be happy in our house, Ivy." Eden sighed.

"Let's stay," Ivy said. "I wanna be a farmer with Mr. Teddy."

Eden saw her daughter wave then, all smiles for the handsome older man waving right back. He was on the phone, talking animatedly. But when his blue gaze met hers, his whole expression changed. It wasn't the first time she'd caught him studying her. Like he was trying to figure something out. Maybe her sleep deprivation was playing tricks on her mind.

"What are your plans today?" she asked Clara.

Clara shrugged. "Teddy... Mr. Boone said he'd take us to the vet hospital. There are some kittens—"

Eden glanced back at Teddy Boone, but he'd turned back to the front desk. She supposed there was a family resemblance between father and son. But Archer was bigger. He didn't smile as easily. Or talk as often. Archer had a thoughtfulness about him—as if everything he did was a clear, intentional choice versus an impulse.

That's why she'd kissed him. Because he'd never kiss her. And last night, she'd wanted to kiss him more than...anything. Her insides turned molten at the memory of him crushing her against him, the strength in his hands and the startling heat of his touch. His groan. Her toes curled.

Her phone was ringing. Again. She'd already let her father go to voice mail three times this morning. They'd had a fight last night. She'd refused to give him editing access to several documents and he'd been livid. Chances were this was more of the same. She had no plans to listen to the messages, and clearly, he wasn't going to give up so...

"Excuse me," she said, carrying her phone onto the front porch. She rounded the corner and answered the phone. "Yes?"

"I've spent the morning on the phone, Eden."

"Leaving messages for me," she jumped in.

"No. Trying to make sure your suite in Palm Springs was upgraded for the girls."

She held her breath, instantly nauseous.

"Are you in Palm Springs?" he asked.

"No."

"Would you like to tell me where in the hell you and my grandchildren are?" he asked, his tone hard as steel. "Because *I* paid for Palm Springs."

She sighed, gripping the wooden railing with her free hand. She didn't want to tell him a thing. She wanted to hand him a well-researched dossier with everything he'd need to convince the board to deny the refuge's funding. That had been the plan. But now...

But now, she wasn't so sure. She swallowed.

"Last we talked you were going to relax, to take a break. Going to Stonewall Crossing was never discussed. Ever." Her father's anger was palpable. "But your credit card indicates you're staying there."

He'd looked into her bank statements? "I am," she agreed.

The silence dragged on, but Eden refused to buckle.

"You've had a hard couple of years, with

work and your personal life. I've been extremely understanding. But my patience is running out."

His *patience*? Her hand tightened on the banister. She would keep her cool, keep it together. "Site visits for every current and potential recipient is something I've done many times. I'm not sure I understand why this is upsetting you. Consider the visit a proactive move on my part." But then, there were things she didn't know. Was that why he was upset? Was he hiding something?

"You may be my daughter, but you're also my employee. If this is a work-related trip, you'd need prior approval before travel. You'd need *my* approval. Something you would not get. What the hell are you up to?" he snapped.

"My job." Spending hours poring over every application, every detail, that was under review each night. She knew her job and what needed to be done. She didn't disappoint or let people down—no matter what he thought. "On all the applications, not just the refuge. But as I'm here, I want to make sure the board has the most up-to-date information."

"Your job, huh?" He paused, his tone sharp when he asked. "This has nothing to do with your mother?"

Eden held her breath. What did he know? What was he keeping from her? Maybe she did want to know why this place was special to her mother. What the people here meant to her. Whatever it was, it upset her father.

"No answer?" Her father's voice was clipped and hard. "Now you're keeping secrets from me."

"And you're not?"

"Oh, I've got plenty. Because I don't want the memories of your momma tarnished."

Eden's heart was thumping in her chest. What did that mean? Her mother would never have been unfaithful to her father. As long as they were married, she'd have honored the vows she made. "What are you saying?"

"Me? I'm not saying a damn thing, Eden. Not a thing." His tone was brittle.

Yes, there were plenty of Clarks in the world. But her mother wasn't one of them. Some people honored their vows. She stared out over the rough country, the greens and browns and bright blue sky so vivid it almost hurt her eyes. "Mom believed in this place. Part of my job—"

"A job *I* pay you to do. That pays for your nanny, your house and your health care. I know you've got some idea that I treat you differently, that I'm harder on you than the rest of my employees—"

"I'm your employee and I work hard for you, *Mr.* Monroe. I have a nanny because you insist I work ridiculous hours, because you give me the hard cases and the difficult people, and I make it work. I earn my paycheck, every hour of every day." She paused, sucking in a deep breath. "Any implication that my paycheck is because I'm your daughter is resented and untrue. I do a damn good job for you, one you should be proud of." She hated the hitch in her voice—hated revealing anything to him.

"Don't come crying to me if you don't like what you find. Your mom's dead. You're not getting any questions answered." He paused. "I'd fire any other employee for doing what you're doing, Eden."

She paused, staring blindly ahead. "Are you saying you'll fire me?"

He sighed. "Guess we'll talk about it when you get back. Got another call," he said, and then hung up.

She stared at the phone, hating the telltale sting of tears in her eyes. So much for finally proving herself to him. Apparently it didn't matter that she was using her own time and money to be here. Or that she was still putting in a full day's work. It didn't matter. He was angry. Over something he wouldn't talk about.

Anger and defeat washed over her. "Bastard," she sniffed.

"He always was." Teddy Boone's voice made her jump. "Your father, I mean. Jason Monroe. And what exactly is your job, Miss Monroe?"

Her cheeks were burning as she said, "I'm a grant administrator and manager for several trusts managed by my father's bank."

"Which means?" he asked, smiling.

"I help decide who gets funding and make sure everything stays in order, for the trusts and the recipients."

"You look just like her," Teddy said. "Same eyes, lighter hair. I knew you as soon as I laid eyes on you."

"But you didn't say anything," she murmured, glancing at him.

"No, I didn't. I don't approve of lying, not one bit. But I know a little about your family. I figure you've got your reasons and will straighten things out when the time is right." He nodded at her. "Question is, why are you here, Miss Monroe?"

"I'm working that out." She stared at him, stunned by Teddy's calm. "I have questions you might be able to answer."

He nodded. "It's not too hot out yet. We could take a walk, if you like?"

She stared at the man. She liked him. But would he tell her something that would change that—and alter the way she thought of her mother forever? Could she blame her mother if…if things had developed between them?

Yes. She could.

She'd never cheated on Clark. Never thought about it. Her word was all she had that was hers free and clear to give. She'd left Clark. She hoped her mother would do the same before she'd move on to another man.

But…she needed to know. She needed to understand her father.

"Ten minutes?" she asked, needing time to pull herself together. And morning hugs from the girls.

"Take all the time you need," he offered. "Just so you know, there's nothing to be said that would prevent your girls and Clara from coming, Eden."

She stared at him for a long time, wondering if that meant that he'd edit his responses or that the niggling fear in her gut was completely unfounded. Either way, she returned to the dining room in time for Lily to start crying. After a long night of teething and lost sleep, it made sense to pack them up for a change of scenery. Better than keeping Clara cooped up with a fussy baby.

She scooped up her daughter, smiling at the giggle her baby made as they spun. "Let's take a walk with Mr. Boone," she said, noting the smile on Clara's face.

In ten minutes, they were strolling along one of the stone-lined paths that made sure visitors didn't stray too far from civilization. Eden cradled Lily, bouncing her or patting her little back to soothe her baby's teething discomfort.

"Poor little thing," Teddy said. "Hurting but no one can fix it."

Eden kissed her daughter's temple, glancing back to see Ivy pointing at the ducks on the pond behind the Lodge. Clara pulled a bag of crackers out and the two of them fed the ducks while she and Teddy wandered a few feet away.

She saw no point in beating around the bush, so she asked, "How do you know my mother?"

"Your mother and my wife, Mags, met in college. They roomed together the first couple of years. Before me and your daddy came along."

Eden looked at him. "And then?"

"Your father is a mite competitive." He grinned. "While your momma was helping me win Mags's heart, he thought I was after Rachel. Don't think he ever let go of that notion, either."

Eden smiled, a hard smile. No, maybe he hadn't. "But you loved your wife."

"Still do." He nodded. "Rachel was a good girl, sweet and funny. She was a good friend to Mags, and to me."

Eden nodded. "She had the best laugh."

"And the two of them together, my Mags and Rachel?" He shook his head. "You heard them laughing, you had to laugh, too."

Eden smiled at him, adjusting Lily against her shoulder.

"We, your dad and me, didn't get on. Went from barely friendly to fighting—I'm not proud of it but it's true." He shook his head. "Made it hard for the ladies to stay friends." He shrugged. "Your mom visited here twice. The first time, your brother was at camp or something, so she came to see Mags. She had a great time, stayed a few weeks and relaxed. Your dad showed up and took her home. Her letters got further apart, but time does that sometimes. Mags missed her." He looked at her. "She came back after Mags died. Helped me with my kids—a houseful of teens hurting. She made them smile, but I could tell she was worn out, tired, sad." He looked at her. "I only asked once why she stayed. She couldn't leave him, she said, didn't want to let you down or drag you through a messy divorce."

Which was exactly what would have happened.

"She said taking care of you was more important than being happy."

Eden swallowed, knowing exactly how that felt. Her babies were the only thing that made her happy. And her father offered the only security she had—hard as he was.

"That's it? You're telling me he wants me to pull the refuge's funding because of some misplaced rivalry?"

Teddy frowned, stopping in his tracks. "Pull funding? Archer'll be torn up over that."

She nodded. Archer lived for his work, for those animals. He loved them unconditionally. He was a good man. A man she didn't want to hurt, not in the least.

Her father. She had no illusions about her father; everything he did had a purpose. Which was smart business, she supposed. But now she knew—deep down—this wasn't business; this was personal.

And it was wrong. Self-loathing rose up, churning in her gut. She didn't care what he said or did; she would do her job. And if Archer's numbers and books checked out the way she knew they would, she'd make sure the board knew it. "I'm going do my job, Mr. Boone. And all that I can to help the refuge."

Teddy stared at her. "Seems to me you're taking a personal interest in this."

She didn't say a word; she couldn't.

"You care about my son." He spoke softly, the way Archer spoke to a frightened horse.

She had no answer for that. Not one she wanted to consider. "I don't believe a person should stand by and watch an injustice happen."

Teddy grinned. "What do you plan on doing?"

She realized they were almost to the refuge. "The board will want irrefutable evidence that Archer has done everything he's set out to do. That the refuge is a worthwhile investment. I'll make sure they know he has."

Teddy's grin dimmed. "And?"

She frowned at him. "This is all business, Mr. Boone."

"Is it? That's why Archer doesn't know who you are?" He was looking at her, intently, his smile slowly returning. "You're just as stubborn as he is." He shook his head, amused.

"Mr. Boone, please. I respect Archer... admire him..." She broke off and drew in a deep breath. She *should* tell Archer the truth. But she was scared. Whatever was between them was fragile. Not that she could let it develop into anything. She couldn't—their lives didn't fit.

She shook her head, hating her roundabout train of thought. As frustrated as she was with her own indecision, she wasn't going to talk to Archer's *father* about it. Instead, she redirected the conversation. "Did my mother want to start an endowment for the refuge?"

He shrugged, his eyes searching hers before he answered. "I think so. I'll see if I can find her letters to Mags."

"Letters?"

"Rachel and Mags wrote regularly. An old-fashioned notion these days." He smiled. "But Mags looked forward to them, like a visit from a loved one."

This was good. And bad. Right now, she had questions without answers. But what if, as her father warned her, she didn't like the answers? There was no way to erase what she learned. "If you can find them," she murmured, hesitant. "Please."

"Momma! Momma!" Ivy called out. "Look!"

Eden turned back to find her daughter running toward her, a huge bouquet of wildflowers in her arms.

She stooped, turning Lily so she could see the flowers. "Look, Lily. Sissy has flowers."

"Si-si-me-me-maw!" Lily squealed, her fist flailing.

"Here." Ivy poked some red and pink flowers into Eden's braid. "Like a princess."

"Three princesses," Clara said, tucking flowers into Lily's hair, as well.

"Four." Ivy jumped up and down. "You, too, Clara."

"Any princesses want to go see some kittens?" Teddy asked.

"You go on," Eden said. "I've got work to do. Have fun." She waved them off, taking her time, enjoying the song of the mockingbird and the wind in the trees. The sun played hide-and-seek with the rapidly moving white clouds in the cornflower-blue sky.

Fester whinnied good morning, making it impossible for her to ignore him. Instead, she stood on the lowest fence rail and welcomed his hug.

"I'm glad you're still happy to see me," she whispered, glancing across the paddock at the barn on the far side.

She looked for him, tall and broad and strong, likely focused intently on something. But a quick sweep of the barn, sheds, pastures and pens…no Archer. She felt hollow—empty. It had been hard before, wondering how it would feel to be held by him. But now that she knew, she ached to be in his arms.

Chapter 8

Archer had been called to the vet hospital early that morning. Another perk of being faculty—emergency duty. It would have been one thing if it was something exotic or unique. But he had no patience for irresponsible pet ownership.

"He's a digger?" Archer asked the two college students who owned the massive mix dog drooling all over the floor. Poor thing wasn't taking the stress well. And the broken leg couldn't be comfortable, either.

They nodded.

"Guess we could tie him in the backyard," one offered.

Archer sighed, shaking his head. "No animal wants to be tied."

They looked at him.

"What are we supposed to do?" the other asked.

"I'm assuming he doesn't have a crate?" Archer asked. "You should get one. He needs a safe place when you can't supervise him. And training. Obedience training. You'd all benefit from that."

One frowned at him. "Isn't that mean? Locking him up?"

"Ideally Bruce would stay in the backyard and out of trouble. But since we know that's not the case, you need to figure out how to prevent this from happening again. A crate or kennel gives them a place to be safe, a place they know means quiet time. With a dog this size you need to make sure you give him plenty of exercise when you're home. And I mean a lot." He nodded at the dog. "He's lucky that driver swerved or he'd be dead."

The boys exchanged a look.

"We offer classes here in the evening. If you adopted him from the local shelter, bring your adoption papers and you'll get a discount. Your college ID will get you another discount." He paused, rubbing the dog's ear.

"He's smart. He'll pick it up quick. Your job will be consistency."

He went over care for Bruce, told them to make a follow-up appointment and went in search of coffee. He headed down the hall, nodding at his brothers Hunter and Fisher before cutting through the recovery room. But he was stopped in his tracks by Ivy, with flowers in her hair, staring at a kitten with pure adoration. Her little hands were curled under her chin, as if she was barely controlling her excitement.

He stopped, surprised, looking around the room for Clara or Eden.

Ivy saw him and smiled. "Hi, Dr. Archer. It's the most prettiful thing I've ever seen," she said to him.

The tiny striped orange kitten seemed equally enamored with Ivy, reaching out a paw for her attention.

"Prettiful?" he repeated.

Ivy nodded, almost nose to nose with the kitten. He could hear the kitten's purr from where he stood. "Think it likes me?"

"Yes."

"I love him," Ivy said.

Archer picked up the kitten, turning it onto

its back. "Her." The kitten mewed pathetically.

Ivy looked perplexed until Archer deposited the kitten in her arms.

"The kitten is a her," he explained.

"Like me." Ivy was all smiles, giggling as the kitten rubbed its head under her chin.

He smiled back. "But you don't have a tail."

Ivy giggled, and the sweet freedom of it washed over him.

"Or whiskers," he added.

She giggled harder. Downright adorable. What had she said? Prettiful.

"Or stripes," she said, still giggling.

He nodded.

"What's she doing?" Ivy asked, bending her head so she could listen to the kitten.

"She's purring," he explained. "Means she's happy."

Ivy tried to purr, giggling again. "I'm happy, too."

"I see that," he said, squatting beside her.

"Can we be farmers, too? I want to stay here." She rubbed the kitten against her cheek. "Momma's happy. She doesn't cry."

Archer felt like he'd been kicked in the gut. "She cries at home?"

Ivy nodded, leaning forward to whisper.

"Grandpa's grumpy and yells. Momma works lots." Ivy's simple honesty tore at his insides.

Eden cries. She feels trapped. She's not happy. But in his arms, she'd come alive. He'd felt it. Maybe this is where she needed to be. He was beginning to accept that's where he wanted her to be.

"Momma needs a kitten," Ivy said.

Archer grinned. "Think it'll help?" he asked.

Ivy tried to purr again.

"A kitten's a lot of work," he said. "Might need to talk to your momma before you take this one home."

Ivy frowned, nodding.

"She's with Archer." His father suddenly appeared and was out of breath.

"Oh, Ivy, we were looking for you," Clara said, pushing Lily in the stroller. "I know you like the kittens, but you must stay with us."

Ivy sighed, her shoulders drooping. "Sorry. She meowed at me."

Archer exchanged a smile with his father.

"Kittens'll do that, Ivy. Especially to sweet, pretty girls like you," his father said. "Let's get you home so you can tell your momma all about the kitten."

"Where is she?" Archer asked.

"Working," his father said.

Archer frowned. Ivy's recent declarations made him wish she were here, enjoying her daughters, instead of poring over his books in a dingy closet-turned-office.

"She knows how important this is, son." His father clapped a hand on his shoulder. "But she didn't eat much this morning." His voice was low.

Archer arched a brow.

"Time is a-wasting, son." His father sighed. "I'd hate for you to let her slip away. Assuming I'm right and you're hoping Eden will stay for more than just bookkeeping purposes?"

But he already knew her answer. She wasn't interested. "I don't think there's much chance of my changing her mind."

"Women are mysterious creatures, son. Might be she's more in your corner than you realize." His father smiled.

Archer stared at his father, waiting for some explanation.

"Just…try." His father's tone was hard. "And be nice. Chasing her off would be the biggest mistake of your life."

"Momma plays chase, too," Ivy offered.

Archer shook his head, smiling at her.

"I'm gonna grill some burgers for dinner,"

his father said. "Why don't you go bring her back to the Lodge tonight? Might take the wagon out for a hayride, too. Look at the stars."

Archer frowned at his father before glancing at Clara. The woman was holding Lily, pointing at the poster that listed all the recognized dog breeds. Lily's little hands and feet kicked and reached, soaking up what Clara was saying softly.

Was this night hayride for her?

He wasn't sure how he felt about his father's new...crush. At the end of the day, it had nothing to do with him. His father had been alone for a long time. When Eden left, Clara would go, too. His father wasn't stupid. If he wanted to set himself up for heartache, Archer couldn't do much to stop him.

As for himself... He didn't know what the hell to do. He'd spent the longest night tossing and turning in his bed. Long after he'd made his way home, he'd felt her mouth on his. She'd been so soft, so eager, against him. And the taste of her, her sweet scent, kept him teetering on the edge of sleep.

He knew she was unhappy.

He knew he wanted her.

Other than that, he didn't know much about

her. How could a man like him, analytical and cautious, give in to something as insubstantial as these feelings?

Ivy's excited squeal stopped all other conversation.

"A hayride? With horses?" she asked.

"Your momma said we have to wait on the horses," Clara said, glancing his way. "They're bigger than the chickens and the baby goats."

"And the kittens," Ivy added, staring longingly at the little orange tabby.

"It's supposed to be a clear night," Archer said, hesitant. "I don't see why we can't go for a hayride. You'll meet plenty of horses. Okay?" Seeing Ivy's smile was a thing of pure delight. He liked that he could make this little girl happy. He wanted to do the same for Eden, to make her smile like that. He may not know much about Eden now, but that was something he could fix.

"Tank you, Dr. Archer," Ivy squealed.

Eden heard the door to the administration offices open and tensed. Would Teddy have told Archer the truth? Would he be furious? His boots echoed off the floor, straight to her door. She didn't know what to feel—excited or anxious. After last night and the phone call this morning, she was a ball of contradictory emotions.

"I brought you something." Archer entered, placing a brown paper bag on the edge of her desk. "Ivy said it was your favorite."

She stared up at him, immediately caught up in his blue gaze. "Ivy?"

"She was at the vet hospital, picking out kittens." He grinned. He was so beautiful her heart thumped.

"A kitten? That's better than a chicken, I guess." Eden picked up the bag and peered inside. "You brought me a pastry?"

"Dad said you had a rough morning, didn't eat." He shrugged. "Not good for you."

She pulled the fluffy pastry, covered in icing and sweet stickiness, from the bag. "I'm not sure this is good for me, either." She smiled.

He shrugged. "Looked good."

"Share it with me?" she asked, standing.

He didn't move. And the space between them grew charged, taut. "You look tired," he said. "I've been pushing you too hard."

She shook her head. "I'm fine. You're the one who looks wiped out." Which was true.

He had dark smudges under his eyes and stubble covering his jaw.

He smiled. "Didn't get much sleep." He cleared his throat.

"Worrying about this?" she asked, tapping the paperwork spread across her desk.

"That's part of it," he answered. "But mostly, I was thinking about you."

She blinked, her heart in her throat.

"Last night shouldn't have happened," he said, his voice gruff. "But it did. And I can't stop thinking about it." He shook his head. "Whatever that was, it doesn't change my offer. I'm serious about the job. About you and the girls starting over here."

She frowned, confused. He hadn't said he regretted it. But he didn't seem happy about it, either. What did that mean? What was he thinking? Feeling? Wanting?

All of which was irrelevant until he knew the truth. She wanted him to know the truth, wanted him to know who she really was before things grew more complicated. Once he knew the truth, he might not be so eager to have her stay. Which was probably for the best. If he didn't want her here, it would be easier to leave—to not find staying here, with him, so tempting. "Archer, there's something I need to tell you."

"Eat first." He cocked an eyebrow. "Meet me out front in a few minutes?"

She nodded, marveling at the smile he shot her way before backing from her office. "Okay," she murmured.

She ate half the pastry, finished her cup of coffee and washed her hands in the sink before walking onto the front porch. A hard and heavy knot of tension rested beneath her lungs, pressing in until she felt sick to her stomach. Archer was waiting, his hands on his hips, staring out at the refuge. She saw him yawn, the slow drag of his hand over his face, and felt a pull of sympathy for him.

He worked so hard.

"Do you ever stop?" she asked, suspecting she already knew the answer.

His gaze settled on her, the corners of his eyes crinkling as he grinned. "I can rest when I'm dead," he answered. "My granddad used to say that all the time. Man never sat still. If he had, we wouldn't be where we are today."

She tore her gaze from his, willing her heartbeat to return to normal. The sun was bright in the massive blue Texas sky, edging the rolling hills in gold.

"Need to check some fences and pens," he said, walking down the steps. "We can talk while I drive."

"I can wait," she offered, her nerves getting the best of her.

"Now's as good a time as ever." He stopped, waving her forward.

She reluctantly followed him to the white truck labeled Boone Ranch Refuge, climbing into the passenger seat as he held the door wide. He smiled at her, those blue eyes so damn bright. She watched him walk back around the front of the truck to climb in. She didn't know how to start. Her words seemed to evaporate before she could actually say them.

They were bouncing through a pasture when he said, "I want to know you, Eden."

She looked at him, stunned by his straightforward admission. "You do?"

He nodded, not looking at her. "I do."

She swallowed. "Even though I'm leaving soon?"

His blue eyes bore into hers. "Even if you leave soon."

"Archer, my father—"

"Your dad is grumpy. Ivy's words, not mine." His voice lowered. "She said you cry a lot."

She tore her gaze from his, staring at her hands. "Ivy's three."

"So she'll tell it like she sees it."

She glanced at him. "My father is a hard man."

Archer turned the wheel, slowing as they approached a gate. "No man should make you cry, Eden. Especially a girl's father." He climbed out of the truck before she could answer. She watched him open the gate with sure motions, all muscle and man. She was breathless and flustered by the time he climbed into the truck and drove through the gate.

"I can get it," she said, needing fresh air. She climbed down and closed the gate behind his truck.

He was smiling when she pulled herself up into the truck. "Thank you," he said.

She nodded.

"Your father." His expression was thoughtful when he looked at her. "Tell me about him."

She sucked in a deep breath. "My father is a businessman. He's used to being in control of…everything. He and my brother are very close. He and my ex-husband are close."

"But you're not?" he asked. "Close to him?"

She shook her head. "No. He's so busy all the time. Too busy for me and the girls. Sometimes I think, to him, I'm more of a...nuisance than a necessity." She saw his knuckles whiten, his grip tightening on the steering wheel.

"Why do you say that?" he asked.

She stared out the window, trying to encompass years of condescension and digs into an accurate explanation. "He's said as much. No matter what I do, it's not good enough. But the more he complains and points out what I do wrong, the more I want to prove him wrong." Her laugh was hard. "Maybe that's his plan. To push me until I get it right?" She felt Archer's eyes on her, but refused to look at him. "He's more bark than bite. The girls and I have never wanted a thing—he's taken care of us. He may not *be* there, but he's all we've got. For that, I'm grateful."

Silence filled the truck cab, so thick Eden felt it pressing in on them. She rolled down her window; the steady hum of the cicadas filled the air.

"Then why not stay here?" he eventually asked, driving slowly along a barbed-wire fence. "You'd be necessary to the refuge."

But not to you? She swallowed.

He parked the truck, looking at her. "We work fine together, Eden. I'd try my hardest to treat you with nothing but respect."

She stared at him, caught up in everything about him. His strong, chiseled jaw. His angular features. The constant intensity in his blue eyes. She should tell him, now. He deserved the truth. Here he was, talking about respect… And she was lying to him.

"Like I said, my life is—" she murmured, so torn.

"Complicated." He nodded. "Doesn't need to be. Life here's pretty simple. Something's broke, you fix it. You do what needs to be done, then what you want to do."

You do what needs to be done.

That was a concept Eden could agree with. She had something very important that needed to be done—she needed to help Archer. She needed to help save the refuge, in whatever small way she could.

"I've had pretty much everything a body needs. Never wanted much." His words wavered ever so slightly, drawing her attention back to him. He was staring at her. "I want you to stay."

Breathe. Just breathe. Keep it together. Her trembling fingers slid over the turquoise stones on her bracelet. He wanted her to stay? For the job? Or was there more to it? She remembered the featherlight brush of his lips on hers and trembled, her gaze falling to his mouth. "Archer…"

He cleared his throat and shook his head. "Don't answer. Just think about it." He smiled as he opened the truck door. "I figure taking a tour of Boone Ranch might help you make your mind up."

He was as good as his word. An hour of driving later, Eden knew that Boone Ranch was beautiful country. Archer wasn't much of a talker, but he shared his family history— how his great-great-grandfather had staked his claim on Texas and how the following generations had done their best to be responsible landowners. She saw the pride on his face, the determination he exuded when he talked about his hopes for the refuge. What would it be like to be part of something so big? Deep roots, solid family, a rich history and satisfaction in a worthwhile job. He wanted her to be a part of that. When he pulled up in front of the refuge offices, he was relaxed. And she was on edge.

She'd had plenty of time to tell him the truth—but she hadn't. She couldn't.

His phone started ringing, giving her the excuse she needed to slip out of the truck. She didn't want to intrude on his phone call. And if she was being honest, she needed to regroup. Her head and heart were at opposite ends of the spectrum this time... But then, how long had it been since she'd listened to anything her heart said? She walked down the path, her mind racing. And hopeful. She'd planned on telling him the truth, but how could she tell him now? Now that she might, possibly, want to stay on the ranch—with Archer. And how could she stay, without him knowing the truth?

Chapter 9

Archer had been staring at the same screen for thirty minutes. He'd read the same paragraph on wound treatments at least six times. The words were in order, it made sense, but Archer had no idea what he was reading. It was late and he was worn out. He'd had another emergency, a house cat that had ended up being the neighbor dog's chew toy. The cat was stabilized, covered with a dozen or more bald patches and sutures.

He sat back and threw his pen onto his desk.

He was angry.

Hurt.

For Eden. Her words tore his heart out.

Life was hard enough without having people on your side. As much as his family drove him crazy, he knew they would drop everything if he needed them. It's what family did—irritated the shit out of one another and took care of one another.

Eden didn't have that. Her girls didn't have that. And that was wrong.

What was he going to do about it?

Was it his place to do anything?

He clicked off his desk lamp and stood, then left his office and headed out to his truck. The sun was disappearing, long fingers of pink and purple stretching across the sky to disappear into the creeping black. He climbed into his truck and headed north, down the country road that brought him to the Lodge.

Two wagons waited, piled high with hay and strung with white lights.

"Didn't know if you'd make it," his father greeted him. "Long day?"

Archer nodded. "You could say that."

"Up for riding sideline?" he asked. "Already got drivers for the wagons."

He nodded. "I'll go saddle River."

"Done," Renata said.

"Dr. Archer." Ivy's little voice echoed down the steps. "See, Momma. He said he'd come." She came running down the stairs.

"I'm coming," Eden's voice was soft.

But Ivy was already at his side, smiling up at him. "Hi. See all the horses?"

He smiled. "I do."

"Momma said to wait for you. I did," she offered, holding up her hand to him.

Warmth flooded him, easing his tension. It was hard to be anything but happy on the receiving end of such an enthusiastic smile. He took her small hand in his, chuckling when she hopped up and down.

"Ivy, please listen to Dr. Archer, okay?" Eden was there, the smile she gave him tight and uncertain. She seemed tense, out of sorts. And it made him sad.

"Which is yours?" Ivy asked, still hopping.

He smiled at Eden, touching his hat in greeting before crouching by Ivy. "I'll show you. But there's a secret to horses, Ivy."

She stared at him, her eyes going round. "A secret?"

He nodded. "They get spooked real easy," he said. "They like whispers and slow movements."

"Okay," she whispered. "I can go slow and be real quiet."

He squeezed her hand. "I know you can. Come meet my horse, River."

"You have lots of horses?" Ivy asked, her little hand clinging to his as they walked to where the horses waited.

"They're not all mine," he said.

"Momma said you take care of all of them," she stated.

He nodded, glancing back at Eden following several steps behind. Her gaze was fixed on the stone path under their feet.

"You a horsey doctor?" Ivy asked.

"A veterinarian," he agreed. "An animal doctor."

"All animals?" she asked.

"Yes." He stopped. "This is River."

Ivy stared up at the red dun he favored. The horse lowered his head, sniffing Ivy's curls.

Ivy clapped a hand over her mouth, stifling her giggle. "What's he doing?"

"Saying hello," Archer answered, loving the sound of her giggle.

Eden's soft laugh reached his ears, drawing his attention. But as quickly as their gaze met, she looked away.

"He's big," Ivy said. "You sit high up."

He nodded, glancing at Eden. "Mind if I put her in the saddle?"

Eden shook her head. "Hold on, Ivy."

Archer sat Ivy in the saddle and swung up behind her. "How's that?" he asked.

"High up," Ivy said, her voice high and thin.

Eden smiled. "You're taller than me, Ivy."

"I am," Ivy agreed, excited again.

It was hard to look away from Eden. She was smiling at her daughter, the sort of smile Archer wanted for himself. He wanted to make her smile. To make her laugh. He cleared his throat. "Going on the hayride?" he asked Eden.

Eden looked at him, shaking her head. "Lily's too fussy to go."

He nodded, disappointed.

"I'll stay here," Clara volunteered. "You haven't had much fun, Eden. You should go."

"Since you and Renata are going with them, son, I'll stay here and make some coffee and cocoa for after," his father offered. "Let's get you and your momma into the wagons, okay, Ivy?"

Archer nudged River forward with his knees and Ivy squeaked. "We're moving," she whispered, loudly.

Archer laughed.

"You're riding a horse," Eden said.

"I am." Ivy nodded. "Can I ride in the wagon, too, Momma?"

When Eden and Ivy were in the wagon, Archer stayed in the saddle, River patiently waiting at the side of the wagon. Ivy asked him questions about horses, what they ate, why they have hooves, how often they need their hair brushed and when their bedtime was. He answered them all, watching Eden's cool demeanor slip further and further away.

"Do they like marshmallows?" Ivy asked.

"Nope." Archer shook his head. "It'd give them a tummy ache."

"Poor River," Ivy said.

The ride wasn't long. They looped down, following the fence, crossing the bridge, then skirting around the refuge and back to the Lodge. He wasn't sure when Ivy fell asleep, but the sight of her sprawled across Eden's lap made him content. About the only thing that could make it better was hearing Eden say they'd stay.

The strands of light cast the wagon's inhabitants in a soft glow. But he saw only Eden. Her fingers stroked through Ivy's curls, her own long hair swaying in the evening breeze.

She was listening to Deacon as he strummed his guitar and sang some classic country tunes.

When they got back to the Lodge, he tied River to the hitching post, then hurried over to lift Ivy into his arms before Eden had a chance to climb down from the wagon.

"Thank you," she said softly.

He stared down at her, wishing he were better with words. He nodded, carrying Ivy up the steps and inside the Lodge.

Eden offered. "I can take her."

"You can get the door," he said, waiting for her to open the door to her suite. Once they were inside, she tugged back the sheets and blanket. He stooped, placing Ivy gently on the bed before Eden covered her with a fluffy pink blanket.

Ivy yawned, gave them a bleary-eyed smile and rolled over. "Night, Momma. Night, Dr. Archer."

"Sweet dreams," Eden said, pressing a kiss to her temple.

Archer felt that strange warmth again. A contentment both new and comfortable. Eden brushed past him to check the crib. Her scent filled his nostrils, stirring every nerve to life.

"Lily's sound asleep," she whispered.

He nodded, still reeling from the effect she had on him. Was this normal? To be so struck by her that thoughts, words and simple actions became difficult? At the moment, he was aware of how alone they were. How good she smelled. How badly his arms—he—ached to pull her close. But first, he needed to know. "Eden?" he whispered.

Her gaze locked with his.

"You've been dodging me all night." His voice was low, soft. "What happened? What changed?"

She shook her head.

He stepped forward, frowning down at her. "Something changed."

"Things… Everything has changed," she murmured.

"It has?" His voice was gruff, anticipation swelling in his chest.

She clasped her hands in front of her. "If I stay, I want it to be for the right reasons."

He couldn't stop his smile. It was involuntary, uncontrollable, and it felt good. Damn good. "What would the right reasons be?"

Her eyes went round, her breathing shallow. "I'm still working that part out."

He stepped back, needing space before he lost his head and gave in to temptation. If he started kissing her, he wasn't going to stop. "Let me know when you've worked it out." He nodded and walked out of the room.

"I need boots," Ivy announced as Eden navigated the stroller through the crowd. The main square of Stonewall Crossing was covered with tents and tables, craft booths and small stages set in each corner for evening entertainment. Market Days and the Labor Day holiday had Stonewall Crossing buzzing with activity.

"Boots?" she asked.

"Lily, too," Ivy said, looking up at her.

"We'll see." Eden smiled at Clara.

"Boots?" Clara shook her head.

"Boots everywhere," Ivy said. "Blue ones and brown and pink and red…" She kept going.

Eden adjusted Lily's sun hat, trying to keep her creamy skin protected.

"At least it's not too hot," Clara said. "And there's a lovely breeze."

Eden nodded. They'd set out after their pancake breakfast to explore before the sun was too high in the sky. She knew Archer wasn't a fan of working weekends, but she wanted to put in a few hours later—preferably during the girls' afternoon nap.

Teddy had warned them it would be crowded, but she hadn't believed him. It took forty minutes to find a parking space. After assessing the crowded brick sidewalks and numerous vendors, Eden put on the front pack and secured Lily, while Ivy was strapped into the less bulky umbrella stroller. But the girls were content, enjoying the Wild West reenactments, clowns and music.

"Look!" Ivy pointed, her feet bouncing up and down. "Animals."

Sure enough, several long-haired goats sat on the courthouse lawn. An old woman in full pioneer regalia was working a spinning wheel.

"What's she doing?" Ivy asked.

"Spinning," Eden said.

"No, she's not spinning, Momma." Ivy grinned up at her. "She's sittin' still. What's she doing with the white stuff?"

Eden and Clara laughed.

"It's called spinning," Eden said as she pushed the stroller closer. "She turning the sheeps' hair into fabric."

"Goats," the old woman said. "Angora goat.

Mohair is soft as silk when it's cleaned and combed right."

"I can comb hair," Ivy volunteered.

The old woman smiled. "I just bet you can."

Eden's gaze wandered over the square while Ivy chatted with the old woman. Stonewall Crossing was like something from a different era. The architecture had been preserved, that was clear. If any of the buildings were new, they'd been held to a strict building design. Soda shops, a hardware store, a ladies' boutique with homemade soaps and lotions, a handful of restaurants, and several clothing shops. And, of course, a boot and hat shop.

If they were going native, boots might be in order.

Let me know when you've worked it out.

She'd lived so long reading into what was said and left unsaid she didn't know how to interpret Archer's parting words. He had left her feeling elated and terrified. Elated because there was a chance he'd made room for her in his heart. Terrified because she could be completely wrong and her heart was going to be shredded. Just because *she* wanted his offer to help to mean so much more didn't mean it did.

And there was still her lie—a lie that woke her up, sweating and breathing hard. Could he forgive her?

"You okay, Eden?" Clara asked.

She nodded. "I want some ice cream."

Clara's smile grew. "Sounds good."

They waved goodbye to the woman and her goats and crossed the street toward the ice-cream parlor.

But the broad shoulders and close-cropped sandy blond hair of one particular cowboy caught her eye. Archer Boone was headed straight for them, a large lizard draped across his shoulders.

Ivy burst into tears.

"What's the matter?" Eden braced the front pack holding Lily with one arm as she stooped by Ivy's stroller.

"It's scary," Ivy said, peeking between her fingers to look at Archer.

"If Dr. Archer is holding it, I bet it's not scary," Eden said. "Isn't that right?"

Archer stopped. "That's right."

She smiled at him, eyeing the dinosaur-esque creature he was holding. "What is it?"

"A friend from the vet hospital." He smiled right back. "A bearded dragon."

Ivy squealed. "A dragon?"

Archer laughed. "A little one. No fire. No wings."

Ivy peeked between her fingers again.

"He won't hurt you," Eden offered.

"Want to touch him?" Archer asked.

Ivy shook her head.

"I can take him back to the hospital booth." It was the first time Eden noticed the large man at Archer's side.

"Booth?" Clara asked.

"We've got animals here for people to see and learn about, part of the veterinary hospital community outreach. Don't blame her. I'm not much of a reptile man myself."

Eden smiled.

"Fisher Boone," the man said. "Archer's younger, smarter and more charming brother."

Archer shot him a look. Eden laughed.

"Hand him over." Fisher took the lizard.

Ivy lowered her hands. "Are you okay, Dr. Archer?"

Archer smiled. "I'm fine. He's friendly, Ivy, I promise."

Ivy crossed her arms over her chest and frowned.

"She's not buying it," Fisher said. "I wanted to meet you, Miss Caraway. And thank you for helping Archer out. He's a hell of a lot easier to live with when he gets his way."

Eden laughed.

Archer sighed. "Just take the lizard back to the booth."

"What kind of ice cream do you want?" Clara asked Ivy.

"Pink," Ivy said. "Please."

"Would you like to join us for ice cream?" Eden asked.

Archer's gaze shifted to her. "Sounds good."

Buying ice cream was an ordeal. The shop was crowded and everyone inside seemed to know who Archer was. While Archer tried his best to remain civil, his discomfort was obvious. By the time they'd found a patch of shade under a tree on the courthouse yard, Archer looked ready to run.

"Not really a people person, are you?" she asked, watching Clara and Ivy blowing bubbles in the kids' section nearby.

He chuckled. "No. Guess not."

Lily lay on her back, wriggling and cooing. She squirmed and wiggled until she'd flipped herself over.

"Did you see that?" Eden asked, all smiles.

Archer nodded, his eyes fixed on her. The

look on his face was soft and warm, made her feel soft and warm.

Lily cooed.

"You did it, little bug." Eden lay on her side, resting her cheek on the grass beside her daughter. "You'll be moving in no time. Keep at it."

Lily rocked back and forth on her knees, her enthusiasm growing with each rock. Eden laughed, offering her more encouragement. But Eden's attention wandered beyond her wriggling baby girl to the man watching her closely. The look on his face was disconcerting. "What?" she asked.

He shook his head.

She sat up, tugging her shirt into place and running a hand over her hair.

"You're beautiful, Eden," he said, shaking his head. "I…like looking at you." He looked away, his face turning stony.

Her heart took flight, flooding her with unfiltered joy. She moved closer to him. His hand rested on the grass, big and strong. She hesitated, then covered his hand with hers. "Do you?"

His blue eyes met hers as he nodded.

"I like it when you look at me…" Her voice was breathless.

He looked at her hand on his. "I don't do this."

She tried to pull back, but he held tight.

"But I'll try," he added, turning his hand over, twining his fingers through hers.

She smiled, happiness welling up in side. "Tell me, Dr. Boone, what do you do for fun?"

He grinned, shaking his head. "Work."

She nodded at the stage in the corner, the telltale sound of a tuning fiddle reaching them. "Dancing?" she asked.

"Requires a partner," he said, arching a brow.

"You have one." She glanced at Lily. "And if Lily turns you down, you can always dance with me."

He chuckled.

"Momma," Ivy said around a yawn. "I'm tired."

Eden glanced at her watch. "Time to head back to the Lodge. Guess you need to get back to help out at the booth?" she asked.

"I can help get the crew loaded up," he said, scooping Lily into his arms.

Lily stared at him, reaching for his face with both hands. She smiled at him, one hand gripping his nose. He ran a hand over her silken curls and tucked her against his chest, taking Ivy's hand in his.

Eden followed, struck by just how appealing a picture he presented. Holding her babies, caring for them, without being asked or bothered. Her heart was beating erratically, longing weighing down her chest. This was what she wanted. Someone who'd care for her baby girls, who'd love them. Who'd love her.

Car seats were buckled, the stroller was put away and Eden found herself lingering on the sidewalk. "See you later?" he asked.

"Miss Eden." Clara's voice was low. "Why not stay? Unless you need a nap?" She smiled.

"I'd like it if you stayed," Archer said.

"You would?" Eden asked.

He nodded.

"Have fun," Clara said, starting the van.

She felt downright giddy. "Guess you're stuck with me."

"Good." His smile warmed her through, confirming what she'd known but been fighting. She had fallen in love with this stubborn, beautiful cowboy.

Chapter 10

Archer was a private man; his business was his business—no one else's. But tonight was different. Holding Eden's hand felt right. If anything, it kept the awkwardness of social situations at bay. People were watching them, but giving them space. When she tugged him onto the dance floor and slipped her arms around his waist, he didn't resist. How could he? She was in his arms, swaying in time to the music, resting her cheek against his chest. She fit, right there, pressed close. Chances were she heard how out of control his heart was. But that was her fault. He'd held on to her until the music stopped and he had no excuse to keep her against him.

It had been a long time since he'd felt carefree. But showing her every shop on the square, sharing stories about his neighbors and his childhood memories, reminded him there was life outside the refuge. Life he should stop and enjoy when he had the opportunity. Like now.

He bought an iced lemonade and a funnel cake and led her to a wrought iron bench beneath a huge Spanish oak.

"That doesn't look very appetizing," she said, eyeing the funnel cake.

"Try it." He offered her a bite.

She leaned forward, opening her mouth so he could feed her. Powdered sugar rained onto her chin, so he held out a napkin.

"Right there," he said, pointing out the sugar. "And there."

She was smiling, laughing—so was he. What more could he want or need?

"This is dangerously yummy," she said, tearing off another piece and popping it into her mouth. He paused, mid-sip, to watch her lick the powdered sugar from her fingertips. "Mmm, sweet. Maybe a little too sweet." She wiped her lower lip with her thumb before sucking her finger into her mouth.

And every lick had his body reacting. Archer was in pain. Sudden, hot, aching pain.

"Archer?" she asked. "Want some?" She offered him a bite, holding her hand out.

She had no idea how tempting she was. A temptation he wasn't going to resist. His fingers encircled her wrist as he stared at the dusting of sugar on her skin. Her skin, coated in sugar. How sweet would she taste? He wanted to find out. He sucked the fried dough she offered into his mouth, letting his tongue slowly trace the dip between her fingers.

Sweet didn't begin to describe it.

He opened his eyes to find her wide-eyed and dazed. Air hissed from between her lips, and her hand fisted in his hold. She made a sound he'd never heard before, an odd muffled choking sound, before standing abruptly and tugging her hand free.

"Eden?" He stood, turning her to face him.

She stared at his mouth, her breathing uneven.

He grinned. "You liked that?"

She kept staring at his mouth.

He tilted her head back, forcing her to

look at him. He hesitated for a moment, then leaned in to press a kiss against her lips. It was featherlight, a whisper of a kiss. But it was enough to send a powerful surge of hunger coursing through him.

She slid her arms around his waist, and he held her, burying his nose in her hair and drawing her scent deep into his lungs.

"What time is it?" she asked.

"Almost nine," he answered. Vendors were rolling down the tent flaps and packing away their merchandise. It was getting late, and Stonewall Crossing was closing up shop. "There's dancing at Cutter's, so most people will head that way."

"I'm done with crowds for the day, if that's okay?" she asked.

He nodded. It was more than okay. He'd rather not share her with anyone.

"What are you thinking?" she asked. "Right now."

He sighed. "I want to be alone with you."

She smiled. "Where do you want to go?" She paused, a small crease forming between her brows. "Where do you live? I know you don't sleep at the refuge. There has to be a place you call home."

He shrugged. "It's a work in progress."

"I'd like to see it."

He nodded, leading her down the dimly lit sidewalks to his truck. He opened the passenger door for her and helped her in.

They drove out of town and headed toward the ranch.

She didn't say anything, so he asked, "What are you thinking?"

"About this place. It's beautiful, Archer, so different from my community of garden homes and the highways of Houston." She glanced at him. "And my family, too, I guess. Missing my mom. Seeing your family together, how close you are..." She paused. "I envy that." He heard the tremor in her voice and reacted.

He slid his hand across the seat, searching for hers. When her hands gripped his, he waited. He didn't know when she'd lost her mother. But he did know how hard that loss was. And he'd had the love and support of his family to help him through that. Who did Eden have? Who held her when she cried? Laughed with her? Shared Ivy's and Lily's milestones? He couldn't imagine this woman being alone. He hoped she wasn't. As long as she wanted to talk, he would gladly listen.

He wasn't quick to anger, but there was no

denying Eden's father rubbed him the wrong way. He didn't need to meet the man to know she deserved better. Archer didn't understand how Eden's father could live with himself, treating his daughter that way. Didn't the fool know his callous treatment was leaving scars? And by the example he'd set, giving permission for others to do the same.

If she'd stay, he'd make damn sure to treat her with nothing but respect.

He didn't say much as they bounced along the rutted road that led to his place. At the top of the butte, his cabin stood. The original structure had been incorporated into Archer's larger creation. His expansion had followed the original style—clean lines, simple details—minus the faulty plumbing and tricky wiring. For all its quirky corners and odd cubbies, the building was solid and safe. It had stayed put through tornadoes, hailstorms and the occasional flash flood.

Eden peered out the front window. "You live here?" she asked. "It's like a living history museum." She pushed out of the truck.

Archer followed, opening the house and turning on the lights.

Eden paused inside, staring around her.

"We call it the Hunters' House," he said.

"When my great-great-grandfather was settling this area, he had groups of friends that would stop over. And since my great-great-grandmother didn't like having a bunch of men underfoot, this was where they went. I guess it was their hangout. You could drink and cuss and smoke and no one cared."

Eden was still investigating.

The original structure wasn't big. Two stories, the upstairs overlooking the downstairs with a balcony-like landing. Since wooden outhouses were inconvenient, Archer had added a long wing off the back, turning the two-bedroom, no-bath home into a four-bedroom, three-bath home. Since cooking over an open fire wasn't Archer's preference, he'd added a nice kitchen to accommodate a large range, refrigerator and other modern conveniences.

But the hand-hewn wooden walls with white clay and ground stone mortar were impressive. He'd done the best he could to preserve the intricate details cut into the window casing, door frames and stair edges. He'd salvaged some original glass panes, thick and bubbled, for the downstairs windows. He was especially proud of the large mantel and fireplace he and his brothers had taken apart, refitted to prevent smoke leaks and reassembled.

"It's amazing," Eden said.

He ran his hand along the mantel, watching her take note of all the details. She'd notice; she was a detail person. Like him.

"I'm thinking the Boones were a hard-working crew. Meaning nothing changes." She smiled at him, moving toward the bookcases that lined the back wall.

"They had to be, as some of the first settlers. A focused, determined crew."

She smiled at him. "Guess some traits are too strong to fade with time."

He grinned. "I consider them both assets." He closed the distance, wanting to be close to her. Wanting to touch her. "A person can't succeed without determination."

"And focus?" she asked.

He liked the soft flush of her cheeks. When she looked at him like this, his body responded. "Very. Some might say obsession. I don't normally get distracted," he murmured, smoothing his hand over her hair, "but you've changed that. So I'll focus on you."

Eden leaned into his hands, so nervous she could hardly breathe. She wanted him badly.

Sex wasn't something she was comfortable with. It was too personal and invasive. She'd avoided it before Clark, but once they were married, she'd tried to relax in bed. It would have helped if he'd been more patient and less criticizing. As it was, being in bed had felt like being in class. In time, she'd become disheartened. Neither one of them seemed truly satisfied when they'd slept together—something he'd used to rationalize his affairs in the beginning.

She hadn't slept with anyone since the night Lily was conceived. The C-section scar from her two pregnancies wasn't too obvious, but she wasn't sure she wanted Archer's level of focus zeroed in on her body. And yet…when his hands were cradling her face and his lips found hers, her fears and worries evaporated. And in their place was only want. And love.

She kissed him back, reveling in the feel of his tongue against hers, the warmth of his breath, the power of his arms as they crushed her against him. She clung to him, her fingers raking through the short hair at the nape of his neck.

His hand slid beneath her cotton blouse, his warm palm on her stomach, his rough fingers stroking her side. She wanted more, to feel more of him. She shuddered and Archer groaned, deepening the kiss until she was dizzy.

Her fingers fumbled with the buttons of her blouse until it hung open. He stared at her chest, breathing hard, while she unbuttoned his shirt and tugged it off.

Archer reached for her, his hand so hesitant Eden thought he was teasing her. But one look assured her he wasn't. He was... mesmerized by her, studying the curve of her breast before carefully cupping the silk-covered weight in one hand. She arched into his hold, the stroke of his thumb across her nipple making her moan brokenly.

His gaze crashed into hers then, his thumb repeating the action.

She shuddered, blowing out a deep breath.

He sat on the couch and pulled her into his lap, facing him. His fingers unhooked her bra, and he stared, his hands hovering close to her free breasts. Such intensity. Such uncertainty. His breath fanned across the sensitized tips, stealing her breath as he buried his face between her breasts. She held him there, running her hands along the muscled contours of his back and shoulders. His mouth latched onto one of her nipples, sucking it deep before flicking the tip with his tongue.

Eden cried out, arching into him. His mouth was heaven. He held on to her, one arm braced around her back, the other hand cupping her breast. She moved against him, wanting his mouth, his lips, his tongue... wanting all of him.

He sat back, twining his hands in her hair and sliding his tongue deep into her mouth. The sensation, chest to chest, was too much. She ground against him, any worries about his want for her vanishing. He wanted her, badly.

He was relentless. Every inch of her was explored, his nose tracing the length of her side. His lips nipping the underside of her breast. His tongue sweeping the line of her collarbone.

"Archer, please," she murmured.

He was breathing hard when he looked at her.

"Make love to me," she whispered.

"I am," he said. "But I want to do it proper."

Eden felt a moment's disappointment. She wasn't feeling proper. She was feeling needy. Here. On the floor. His truck. Whatever. But she needed him. Now.

"Eden?" he asked.

She blinked.

"Bed," he said, pointing at a hallway.

She slipped from his lap and stood. He was gorgeous. All hard muscle and angular planes. Thick arms, strong hands, a light dusting of hair across his chest. He was the most amazing thing she'd ever seen.

And he wanted her.

He stayed where he was, his gaze traveling over her slowly, leisurely. She fought the impulse to cover herself. He liked what he saw, she could tell. And that made her feel incredibly beautiful. And sexy. She unbuttoned the waist of her gray capris and slid them down her hips. They fell to the ground, leaving her in a pair of light blue lace panties and nothing else.

Archer's hands fisted at his sides, and he leaned forward and reached for her.

His lips brushed her hip; his hands slid along the dip of her back and cupped her buttocks. She gasped, the air shoved forcefully from her lungs. She was ready, hungry.

She stepped back, grabbing his hands and tugging him to his feet. She kept moving. If he wanted a bed, she would find one. When she'd found his room, she let go of him, crossed the wooden planked floor, and climbed onto the white linen–covered bed.

She sat, watching him kick off his boots, toss his socks and wiggle out of his jeans. His boxers joined the pile, leaving nothing to her imagination. Breathing was a challenge. Her body tightened, aching for him. He was a big man. Big and strong and hers.

He crossed the room, leaning over her until she lay back on the mattress.

His hands smoothed down her stomach, gently sliding her panties off.

The mattress dipped beneath his weight as he settled between her legs. He kissed her, his tongue tracing the seam of her lips. She ran her hands over his back and hips, opening her mouth for him.

He smoothed the hair from her face, his gaze holding hers. He cradled her, those blue eyes boring into her—searching her. Her hands moved to cover his.

When he thrust slowly into her, his eyes closed briefly. A low groan caught in the back of his throat. Her moan was soft, stunned. The shock of it, joining physically and mentally, was powerful. She couldn't look away, overcome by the intensity of his gaze and the feel of him deep inside. His jaw locked, a tremor shaking his body as he slid home. "Eden." Her name was broken and gruff. His hand stroked her cheek as he pressed a soft kiss to her lips. He paused, their ragged breaths the only sound.

In that moment, Eden felt truly beautiful. Something about Archer, normally guarded and controlled, vulnerable in her arms, tugged at her heart. He saw her, wanted *her*. And she felt it.

He moved deeper, the control on his face wavering as he pressed his eyes shut, groaning. He shook his head and smiled at her.

His rhythm was slow and deep. He was in no rush. His hands, his mouth, seemed intent on driving her out of her mind. And he was succeeding. Each thrust, each kiss, each whisper of his breath on her skin was sweet torture. Whatever gave her pleasure he explored in depth.

"You're beautiful." His words were as potent as his hands. She felt her body tightening around him. His hand cupped her breast, his thumb grazing over her nipple, his lips and tongue stroking—and she was done.

Her climax hit hard, her cry echoing in the room, her body bowing off the bed. She held on to him, needing an anchor as she slipped into a state of pure bliss. He powered into her then, his face crumpling as he moaned long and loud. His hands gripped her hips as he kept moving, his body shaking beneath her hands.

When he collapsed at her side, they lay there gasping.

"Stay," he said, draping an arm across her stomach.

She rolled onto her side, facing him. He was gorgeous. His eyes were closed, his lips parted. The rapid rise and fall of his chest made her smile. It was more than a little empowering to know she made him breathless. She ran a finger along his forehead, down his nose, across his lips, chin, neck and shoulder.

He turned his head toward her on the pillow, but she continued mapping his body with her fingertips. Sharp edges and broad contours of his chest. She'd known he was in shape, but his body was an unexpected delight. When her fingers stroked across the plane of his stomach, his skin quivered.

Her gaze met his. "Thank you for today," she said.

"Thank you?" His brows rose, a small smile tugging at his lips.

"Yes, thank you." She grinned, feeling foolish as she stammered, "It's been a long time since... No one's ever made me...wanted to... make me feel special."

He frowned.

Her smile faded.

His fingers smoothed her hair from her shoulder. "You are special."

She scooted forward, resting her chin on his chest and draping her arm across his stomach. She liked being close to him, feeling his warmth, breathing in his scent. She sighed.

His arm slipped around her, his large hand pressed open against her back. "Will you stay?"

She rested her cheek against his chest. His heart beat slow and steady, calming enough to lull her into sleep. "I can't, Archer," she said it as much for herself as him. She wanted to stay. Right now, there was nothing she wanted more than to stay right here tangled up in him. "You know I can't."

He stiffened beneath her, his arm falling away as he moved to his side of the bed. He stood, giving Eden a view she couldn't help but admire. Except he was upset. And she didn't know why. "Archer?" She sat up, pulling the sheet over her.

He ran a hand over his face. "I don't bring

women back to my house, to my bed…" He broke off.

She smiled, unable to squelch the pure happiness his admission stirred. But he knew she had children, knew it was complicated. "I want to stay, Archer. But if Ivy and Lily wake up and I'm not there, Clara will have a revolt on her hands."

He turned, wearing an odd expression. He ran a hand over his face and nodded, his posture easing slightly. "I'll take you back."

Eden waited, wishing there were some way to rewind the last two minutes and undo whatever it was that had changed the air between them. He'd been gentle and responsive, like he wanted her here, like she was special. Now he was tugging on his clothes and tight-lipped, like he couldn't wait to take her home.

Chapter 11

Eden took the box Teddy Boone handed her.

"This is all of them. Mags never took to email, so she and Rachel were pen pals."

Eden nodded, truly thankful.

"Don't have the heart to go through her things, so they're all in the attic," Teddy mumbled. "Glad it's of some use."

Eden paused, glancing at Teddy Boone. This man had been alone, grieving for his wife, for almost a decade. Her father had married Julia six weeks after her mother's death. Julia, the midlife crisis cliché. Young, gorgeous and dumb. At least she was sweet. "Guess I need to read through them all."

Not exactly the way she'd been planning on spending her Sunday, but time was running out. "I guess I'm a little scared," she confessed. "I know my parents' marriage wasn't perfect, but there are some things a daughter doesn't want to know."

"Archer's not gonna help?" Teddy asked. "Lot of letters in there."

"I… I couldn't tell him," she murmured.

"I imagine the words get stuck." Teddy sighed, his nod slow. "But soon, I hope? Won't get any easier."

She nodded. Soon. She had to tell him. Now that she loved him. She swallowed. But Archer was nowhere to be found this morning. He'd dropped her off without saying much. Eden had kissed him, but he'd seemed almost disinterested—as if the passion they'd so recently shared never existed. And it scared her. She hadn't known him long enough to know what was going on inside that head of his. But she wanted to. She wanted to know what he was thinking, to understand him.

"I was hoping things were falling into place with you two." Teddy shook his head. "I admit, I'm more than a little disappointed."

Eden glanced at Teddy Boone. "Not all of

us will have a successful holiday romance, Mr. Boone."

Teddy smiled. "Who said anything about a *holiday* romance, Miss Monroe?"

She carried the box to her room and played with the girls. Lily was in love with peekaboo, and Clara and Ivy had just found a new coloring book full of kitten pictures. They went through two purple crayons before Ivy decided she wanted to play peekaboo, too.

She glanced at Clara, sitting on the floor, smiling at the girls. Would she lose her? Could she blame Clara for wanting love? No, she couldn't. And if Teddy Boone was going to make an honest woman out of her, Eden would be happy for her.

She wished it were that clear-cut with Archer. She loved him. She wanted to stay. Considering she'd been here six days, she knew that was insane. But...irrefutably true. She had no idea how he felt about her. He wanted to help her. He was attracted to her. But that didn't mean he was ready to tie himself to her—and her two children, ex-husband and controlling family.

Eden waited until nap time to tackle the box. At first, she felt as though she was intruding, reading her mother's secrets. But it soon felt like she was visiting with her, her voice ringing from each clearly scripted line. She and Mags had been close. And even though she didn't have Mags's letters, it was easy to pick up the thread of conversation between them.

They exchanged stories about their children, their hopes and dreams for them. Their husbands. She was sad to learn that her creation had resulted from an attempt to save her parents' marriage. Like Lily. She was so engrossed that she was completely unaware someone was speaking to her until he tapped the letter in her hand.

"Earth to Eden." Clark smiled, his bright eyes crinkling at the corners.

She stood, stunned. Clark was here? "What are you doing here?"

"I have today and tomorrow off. I felt terrible about canceling on the girls and thought I'd spend it with them." He paused. "Since it's still my week with them."

"So Dad sent you?" she asked.

He shook his head, chuckling. "You're so cynical."

She crossed her arms over her chest. "Not going to answer the question?"

"Your dad is very concerned," he said.

"You realize how pathetic this is, right?" she asked.

He shrugged. "He's the boss."

Eden studied him. "Where are you staying?"

"Here," he answered. "I'm supposed to do a cursory site inspection while I'm here."

She blew out a deep breath. "*You* are?"

He nodded. "Come on, Eden. You have to admit, you coming here like this wasn't the smartest move. Your dad's making it sound like you're emotionally compromised—because of your mother and this place."

"That's not true." Her mother wasn't the problem. It was Archer.

"I know you take your work seriously. I know you wouldn't let anything get in the way of facts and research—emotions or otherwise. I know that. I know you. But your dad…" He broke off, shrugging. "You know how he is."

Eden frowned at him. "Would it kill you to tell me your visit here has nothing to do with the girls and everything to do with staying on my father's good side?"

He had the decency to look uncomfortable. "Where are the girls?"

"They're sleeping."

He glanced at his watch. "Nap time." He glanced at the box full of letters. "They sleep while you're *relaxing*. You look tired."

She smiled. "I didn't get much sleep last night." And it had been wonderful. Well, part of it had been wonderful.

"Lily have a rough night?" he asked.

"She's teething." She saw Teddy Boone peek around the door, watching them curiously. "I'll let Clara know you're here so you can have the girls when they wake up."

He nodded. "Good to see you, Eden." He picked up his bag.

She didn't answer. She waited until he'd left before packing the letters back into the box. She carried them to the front desk. "Teddy," she said. "I need your help."

"Name it."

"Can you tell me where Archer might be?" she asked. "I need to talk to him."

"There's a few places." Teddy sighed. "I'll get Jenny to cover the desk and go look for him."

She shook her head. "I don't want to cause trouble."

Teddy looked beyond her. "That city fellow a problem for Archer?"

"Could be." She nodded. "He's here about the refuge. My father sent him. I want to give

Archer a heads-up." She glanced at the clock. "I need to get into the refuge to finish the paperwork."

"I'll go look for him. Deacon's got keys. He can let you into the office." Teddy patted her hand. "It'll be fine."

"I hope so, Teddy. I can't shake the feeling that my involvement is making things ten times worse."

"I think my boy might disagree with you," Teddy said, smiling.

She hoped he was right.

Archer spun the wrench, wiping the sweat and oil from his fingers to get a better grip. He'd been working on the tractor engine for an hour, cut up two fingers, and the damn thing was still choking. But he wasn't about to give up. Right now he needed straightforward problems with logical answers. Animals. Machinery. Paperwork.

As long as he wasn't thinking about Eden, he was fine.

But even when he wasn't thinking about her, he was. Yesterday had changed every damn thing. He'd never thought all that much about a person's smile or voice or wanted someone's company. He was a solitary sort, always had been. But spending time with her, he'd been fascinated by everything. Stonewall Crossing had been a different town, a brighter place, when she was at his side.

And last night. The feel of her. The taste of her. Watching her come alive and fall apart from his touch… There was nothing straightforward or simple about the feelings she'd inspired in him.

He wanted to keep her beside him, to never let her go.

Another part needed to cut and run—to get as far from her as possible before he begged her to stay. He couldn't be that man, ruled by emotion. He wasn't wired that way. He was cautious, methodical.

Eden challenged that. She made him think that maybe giving in to his heart wouldn't be such a bad thing.

But giving in, loving her, was too big a risk. When she'd said she couldn't stay, he'd thought she'd meant in Stonewall Crossing. And it had hurt. It had been eye-opening. None of what was happening made sense. It wasn't practical or rational. And, damn it, what sort of father would he be to her girls? He shook his head, rubbing his hands on the work rag before tossing it into the toolbox.

The sky rumbled, drawing his gaze upward. The clouds flickered with lightning, thunder bouncing off the hills. Good damn thing, too; they needed rain. The tanks were getting low and the sun was getting hotter. A good soaking would bring welcome relief all around.

A dust trail kicked up, headed straight for him. His father's truck.

He sighed, wiped his hands again and dropped the wrench into the toolbox.

"Archer." His father climbed down from the ranch truck. "I know you're not wanting to be found, but Eden was looking for you."

Archer took a deep breath, fighting the instinct to drop everything and go to her.

"Figured you'd want to know. Since you won't answer your damn phone."

"What's wrong?" he asked, his gut tightening.

Teddy shrugged. "Can't say for sure, but she's pretty upset. She went to the refuge, fired up to finish that paperwork."

Finish that paperwork. A coldness seeped across his skin. She couldn't leave. He might have been an ass last night, panicking about what he could offer her and the girls. He needed to sort through that, talk to her. But she couldn't leave. "She's at the refuge?" Archer asked, eyeing the clouds overhead.

"Told Clara she'd be late and headed out," his father said, peering under the hood. "Giving you trouble?"

Archer nodded. If Eden was upset, then there was a reason. "Dad—"

"Take the truck. I'll ride River back." He offered the keys without looking his way. "Might see if I can get this started before the storm hits, though."

"Thanks. Don't wait too long." Archer headed to the truck, smiling at the sight of his father fiddling under the hood. He put the truck in Reverse, cut across the field and headed toward the refuge.

The closer he got, the more clear things became. It wasn't about needing her help with funding anymore. If he had to dust off his suit and start schmoozing other foundations, he would. He'd figure things out; he always did. Losing Monroe was a shame, but nothing life-altering. But Eden. Well, now that he'd found her, he couldn't comprehend losing her.

By the time he was parking, the rain had started. A quick look told him Deacon and the men had things under control, so he headed inside and shook the rain from his hat before hanging it on the hat rack on the wall.

The lights flickered, followed by the sound of Eden's muttered, "Shit," at the end of the hall.

He smiled, heading that way.

She was feeding things into the scanner, tidy stacks of clipped receipts and invoices arranged on her table. But the power surge must have shorted the scanner because she was tapping it with barely suppressed anger. "Work," she snapped. "Come on."

Her hair fell around her shoulders; her white T-shirt and fitted black pants reminded him of just how heavenly her body felt. Soft and warm and sweet. She'd be one hell of a distraction if Toben saw her now. She turned the machine on and off, then bent to check the plug. Archer adjusted his pants, his jeans increasingly uncomfortable.

He cleared his throat. "Might need to check the breaker."

She jumped up, knocking her head on the shelf mounted to the wall.

"Eden." He crossed the room, taking her hand and edging her under the light. He tilted her head, lifting the hair at her temple. "Bumped it good." His hand strayed to her cheek, distracted by her silky skin against his palm. "I didn't mean to scare you."

"I'm fine," she murmured, leaning away from his touch. He saw the hurt in her eyes, before she turned away.

"This can wait," he said.

The lights flickered again.

"No, Archer, it can't." She stared at him, her expression shuttered—cold. She shook her head, flipping the power button on the scanner. She tapped the machine again, then flopped into her chair and rubbed her head. "That really hurt."

"You should ice it," he said.

"I'm fine," she argued, rubbing her temple.

"If it hurts—"

She held up her hand, her attention shifting to the items covering her desk. "Everything's done. I just need to scan it and upload it all. There's no arguing you've been fiscally responsible. I've collected character statements from people at the state Agriculture Department, the Healing Horseshoe Therapy Ranch, the vet hospital… Anyone you've worked with the last year." She glanced at him. "You're not asking for too much, Archer…"

"Eden, breathe," he said, stepping closer, but she shook her head. She pressed her hand to her temple again, wincing, and he headed for the freezer. He returned, carrying an ice pack. She glared at him, but he didn't budge. She took it, wincing when she pressed the cold to her temple.

"Careful," he said, hating to see her in pain.

She looked at him, her chin wobbling. "I'm so sorry."

"You've nothing to be sorry for," he said, wanting to touch her, to hold her. She'd already shrugged out of his hold once, she didn't want his touch or his comfort.

"I do. I've put an even bigger target on the refuge. My...rebelliousness will hurt you." She shook her head, her gaze meeting his. "I messed things up and I'm sorry."

All he could do was stare at her. And the longer he stared, the more confused he became. How had she put a target on his back? What had she messed up? The paperwork? Right now, he didn't give a shit about the paperwork.

She stood, wiggling the cord on the back of the scanner. "If this would just work—"

His hand closed over hers. "Eden."

She froze.

"I don't know what's got you riled up, but I know it's going to be okay. The refuge will survive without the Monroe funding, don't you worry. We'll figure it out." He placed her hand on his chest. "You..." He shook his head. "You're what matters to me. You're brave—fearless, even. And you make me feel... Feel."

She blinked.

"I started this week worrying about money and the refuge, the horses, life. And now all I can think about is keeping you here." He swallowed. "Even though I know there's no way in hell it makes any sense." He blew out a deep breath.

Her hand tightened on his shirt, gripping the fabric. "It doesn't. We're..."

"Complicated," he said, nodding.

"I n-need to tell you something that will make everything even more complicated." Her voice wavered as her hand slid from his chest. "And you don't do complicated."

"I think I'd do just about anything for you, Eden." His voice was rough, revealing how hard this was. It would be easier if he could tell her, if he could manage to say the words. Instead he kissed her, softly. His hands were gentle, cradling her against him, asking for permission.

"Archer?" Renata's voice rang out. "Archer?" And she was upset.

"In here," he called back, heading down the hall.

"Archer, where's Dad?" Her eyes were huge, brimming with tears. "River just tore into the yard, but the saddle's empty."

He fought back the panic, the crushing fear that gripped him. "He was in the north field. I'll go."

He ran into the rain, ignoring the blinding flash of lightning as he climbed into the truck and slid out of the yard.

Chapter 12

Eden paced the floor, bouncing Lily. It was after ten and she hadn't heard a thing. She'd sent Clara to the hospital, knowing that's where she needed to be.

Lily hiccuped, still sniffling.

"She's having a hard time," Clark said.

Eden nodded. Her tension wasn't helping Lily's fragile state, she knew that. But Archer's face, the fear in his eyes, had haunted her mind since he'd left the refuge.

"Ivy didn't do this." He paused, looking at her. "She didn't, right? I mean, I don't remember this."

Eden shook her head. "No, Ivy didn't cry much."

"Didn't think so." He seemed relieved. "What can I do?" he asked.

She shook her head.

"Do you need to go to the hospital?"

"I don't know," she whispered. "I don't want to intrude."

"But you want to be there?" he asked.

She nodded.

"You like this Archer guy, don't you?" he asked. "His family?"

She patted Lily, avoiding eye contact with her ex-husband. They'd always been friends. He was a nice guy, charming and easygoing—on the surface. But Clark was also an opportunist. His top priority was taking care of himself, even at others' expense. If he learned something interesting, he'd file it away until it could be useful. That, and his cheating, had made it impossible to sustain a trusting relationship. And yes, he'd heard her earlier conversation with Clara—as veiled as it was—but she didn't feel like baring her soul to him. Especially when she had yet to tell Archer just how much she loved him. Or who she really was.

She ached for him. And now, hurt for him.

"I can take care of the girls," he offered.

She shot him a look.

"Okay, take Lily. I can handle Ivy."

She shook her head, smiling. "She's asleep."

"Yeah, I got this." He grinned.

She hesitated. "Are you sure?"

"I'm her dad, Eden. I might not be the best dad, or anywhere in the top hundred, but I do love her." He rubbed his hand over Lily's head. "Both of them."

She nodded. "Okay. I'll take my phone."

"I'll crash on your bed?" he asked. "Since Ivy's already sleeping—I'd hate to disturb her."

She nodded, packing supplies into Lily's diaper bag before buckling her into her seat. She fussed, but there wasn't much Eden could do. She loaded Lily's seat in the car and drove carefully, the storm still raging.

She wasn't family, and she didn't want to intrude, but she needed to make sure Archer was okay. That Clara was okay.

And Teddy.

It had taken thirty minutes to find him. Toben had stopped by long enough to let her know Teddy had been found and a neighbor was using his helicopter to take him to

the hospital. They assumed River had gotten spooked by the storm and thrown Teddy.
He'd been found, unconscious, in a field. And
until the patriarch was talking, it was the only
thing they'd come up with.

She drove through the rain, using her GPS
to guide the way. After she'd parked, she held
Lily close and ran through the downpour.

She stood inside the lobby, adjusting Lily
under the blanket she'd covered her with, and
glanced around. It was a small hospital. But
then, Stonewall Crossing was a small town.
She approached the desk but hesitated, knowing she wasn't family and she'd probably get
turned away.

"Eden?" It was Toben, carrying a tray of
coffee cups. Deacon followed, equally cof-
fee-cup-laden.

"Hi," she said. "I… I wanted to see if I
could do anything."

"About time you got here," Deacon grumbled. "Follow me."

She frowned at Deacon but followed him
through two swinging doors and down a blin-
dingly white hallway to the waiting room
packed wall-to-wall. Faces, some familiar,
others not, regarded her with mild curiosity or disinterest. They didn't care who she

was; they all wanted to know one thing: Was Teddy okay? The level of love and concern in that small room was palpable.

"He's in the hall," Deacon said.

Eden headed in the direction Deacon pointed, turning the corner to find him. Archer. He leaned against the wall, hands shoved in his pockets, head back and eyes closed. Totally still, shutting out the world—wanting to be alone.

Lily hiccuped. Again. And again.

Archer's eyes opened, a small smile forming on his lips as he looked her way. He straightened, pulling his hands from his pockets and flexing them. It was the look on his face—defeat, fear and sadness—that made her go to him.

She didn't hesitate, but slid her free arm around his waist and pressed against him—as much as possible with Lily between them. His arms wrapped about her, supporting Lily's weight while keeping her close. His sigh was deep and slow, but his hand gripped the back of her shirt, pulling her closer.

"What can I do?" she murmured against his chest. "Do you know anything?"

"He was unconscious when I found him. Don't know if he was thrown or fell…" His words were muffled against the top of her head. "Good damn thing it had been raining. Mud made his landing a little softer."

Lily peeked up from under her blanket then, shooting Archer a sleepy grin. Her little fingers reached up to stroke his chin.

Eden looked up to see him smile at Lily with love. He shifted, cradling Lily across his chest and tucking her blanket around her. "Bedtime, little bug," he said, using Eden's pet name. "Sleep now." His voice was low and soft.

Lily burrowed in, yawned, smiled another sleepy smile at Archer and shut her eyes.

Eden's heart was so full of love. And being near him only reminded her of how important he was to her.

"Your shirt is wet," he murmured, sliding his fingers through her hair. "And your hair."

"It's raining," she said, unable to look away from the blueness of his gaze.

He frowned.

"I wanted to be here." She paused, searching his gaze. "I needed to."

He leaned forward until his forehead rested against hers. "Needed."

She nodded.

He nodded, too.

"You don't want to sit? Some coffee? Something?" she asked. "She gets heavy after a while."

Archer glanced at Lily, smiling. "She's fine."

"Archer." Toben waved him forward. "The doctor."

Eden followed. Archer reached back a hand for her, and Eden held tight. All she could do was hope and pray Teddy would be all right. He was fit and strong and, according to Archer, stubborn…all things working in his favor.

"Everyone here now?" the doctor asked. At Archer's nod, he continued, "I'm Dr. McBride. I think most of you know me. And I know your father, so let's cut to the chase. He took a hard fall, knocked his head. We've already run a preliminary CT to check for any subdural bleeds. So far, he looks good. A concussion, to be sure, but we'll know more shortly. He's started to come around, and he's disoriented and crotchety."

That made the waiting room relax; a few people laughed.

"That's a good sign," Fisher, the Boone brother she'd met, said.

Dr. McBride nodded. "It is indeed. I plan

on making him a whole lot more crotchety through the night. We'll do another CT in about twelve hours. Make sure it's clear."

"What are you looking for?" a young woman asked, someone Eden didn't know.

"Any injury to the brain, swelling, that sort of thing." He held his hands up. "Let's not worry about that unless we have to."

"When can he go home?" Renata asked.

Dr. McBride shook his head. "Not for at least twenty-four hours, Renata. With that hard a knock to the head, I'd feel better having him closely monitored for a solid two days. Just to be sure."

Eden squeezed his hand.

"Nothing else?" Archer asked.

"So far, no." Dr. McBride shook his head. "That's all I can tell you right now, Archer. You all let him know you love him, remind him he's here for a reason—and he needs to listen to his doctor, won't you?"

Renata nodded, patting the man on the shoulder. "Thank you."

Lily wriggled, prompting Archer to bounce her without thought. "Can we see him?" he asked.

"For a minute," Dr. McBride said. "I mean

a minute, too. Just the kids, or it'll take an hour to get everyone out of here."

Archer nodded.

She hurt for him, knowing how badly he wanted to see his father. And how hard it was for him to keep up the cool, distant facade everyone seemed to expect from him.

"Here." She moved in close, shifting Lily into her arms. "Give him a kiss from me," she said.

He nodded, smiling down at her. "Can do."

She stepped back, patting Lily to keep her sleeping. But Archer stayed at her side, waiting for his siblings to join him.

"We haven't met. I'm Hunter. The oldest," he said, smiling. "The giant one is Fisher. You know Archer and Renata. And this is Ryder, the baby. You must be Eden."

She nodded. "I'm sorry we're meeting under such circumstances."

"Dad's tough," Ryder stated. "He's probably looking for some sympathy from his new girlfriend."

The siblings smiled.

"Where is Clara?" she asked.

"Dad woke up and wanted her," Renata said, shrugging. "He gets what he wants."

Eden smiled.

"Be back," Archer said.

"I'll wait." She kept patting Lily's back, trying not to react to the head-to-toe inspection by each and every member of the Boone family.

"Who knew you had it in you?" Ryder said, clapping Archer on the shoulder.

Archer scowled at his little brother.

"We're happy for you," Hunter exclaimed, smacking Ryder on the back of the head.

Archer ignored their teasing and followed the nurse. For once, he didn't mind the picking. They were all so relieved their father was okay. Because if there was one thing they all agreed on, it was how much they loved their father. He was their rock, their cornerstone, a constant in their daily lives.

Even catching his father mid-kiss didn't rattle Archer. Hell, his father had a right to be kissing Clara. He should have someone to kiss every day, to smile with, talk to and laugh with.

"Oh." Clara jumped up, blushing.

Their father was grinning ear to ear. "If I'd known this was the way to get kisses from a beautiful woman *and* all my kids in one place at the same time, I'd have nose-dived off a horse years ago."

"Daddy." Renata laughed, moving to the other side of the bed to drop a kiss on his cheek. "No more diving. We'll be better about getting together."

"I'll take that as a promise." He patted Renata's hand.

Archer stood at the foot of the bed, trying not to get hung up on the IVs, the beeping heart monitor or thick white bandage wrapped around his father's head. "You hurting?" he asked, sitting on the end of the bed. He patted his father's foot, resting his hand there, the slight contact enough to ease Archer's lingering worry.

"My back, a little," he said. "My head." He smiled. "Guess that goes without saying."

"What happened?" Hunter asked.

"Don't know. Can't remember much."

Archer sat, content to watch his father and siblings. The quick banter and gentle teasing. His father might be bruised and bandaged, but he looked happy. Patting Clara's hand on his shoulder, laughing at Fisher's story—Fisher always had stories—Ryder's quick comebacks, and Renata and Hunter taking turns shushing them all and telling them to behave.

"I'm only going to say one thing." His father drew in a deep breath. "We need to be better about making time for this family. All of us, so these babies know their roots and they're loved. You hear me?"

They all mumbled agreement, a long awkward silence stretching out before Hunter asked, "You like Archer's gal?"

"You missed it." Ryder paused, holding up his hands. "Archer was holding a baby. A *baby*."

Archer sighed, running a hand over his face.

"She's a very cute baby," Renata said.

"She is that," Clara agreed, smiling at him. "So is her momma."

Archer grinned.

"She here?" his father asked.

Archer nodded.

"She was worried about him." Fisher nodded in Archer's direction. "I'm sure she was worried about you, too, Dad."

The others laughed.

"I'm fine with her worrying about him. He needs someone to worry over him." His father smiled.

"Okay, that's a wrap." Dr. McBride came

in. "It's late. You need rest. And there's far too many children up past their bedtime in my waiting room."

"Come on now, Rupert," their father argued. "You can't tell a man his grandkids are here and not let him see them. Bad for a man's heart."

Rupert McBride shook his head. "You can see them tomorrow. If you behave tonight."

His father frowned. "Now hold on—"

"Dad," Archer interrupted. "Getting worked up isn't going to change his mind."

His father frowned at him, then Dr. McBride. "Fine."

The five of them hugged and kissed their father before leaving the room.

"She's not going anywhere," Archer heard his father arguing with Dr. McBride.

He smiled, returning to the waiting room. Eden sat, rocking Lily, talking with his brother's wives. It was a cozy picture, one that struck him as right. He wanted her to fit with his family, to find friendship and love here. And his brother's wives were good women—as far as women went.

She saw him and smiled. "How is he?"

He nodded. "Good. Don't think you'll be getting Clara back tonight."

She laughed.

"We have to come back tomorrow," Hunter said. "He wants all of his grandkids under one roof."

"We need to work on that." Renata shook her head. "We live in the same town, a small town at that. How hard would it be to get together once a month?"

The idea of regular family gatherings didn't appeal to Archer. But if it would make his father happy, he'd do it. Nothing had prepared him for the terror he'd felt driving through the rain. He couldn't find him. And every minute was one more minute his father was missing, hurt, bleeding... Seeing him in the mud, still and pale... He shivered at the memory. He'd slammed the truck into Park and dropped to his knees in the mud, frantic until he'd found a pulse.

Hunter had already called Caleb Brewer, a friend with a helicopter. It might normally be used for counting and tracking the white-tailed deer and exotics that lived on the ranch, but it had doubled as an ambulance. Archer had used plywood, a saddle pad and tie-downs to secure his father's neck before they moved him into the helicopter. Seeing his father gray and lifeless… He shook his head. "I can do once a month."

His brothers nodded.

"When he gets released," Renata said. "At the Lodge?"

Archer glanced at Eden. He wanted her to be there, a part of this—his family. Maybe she wouldn't go if he told her how he felt. Hell, telling her to stay and offering her a job wasn't the same thing as asking her to stay—with him.

"You ready to go?" he asked.

"I've got my van," she said, standing.

He shook his head. "I'd like to take you. We'll get the van later."

"Thank you." Her smile was a thing of beauty. "Now?"

He didn't realize his family was watching him. Until he tore his gaze from Eden's. Every single one of them was staring. Even the kids. He sighed. "Now's good."

"It was nice to meet you all. I'm so glad he's going to be okay." Eden gave smiles, hugs and handshakes to the whole damn room before he managed to get her to himself.

It was only as he was moving Lily's car seat into his truck that he realized someone was missing. "Where's Ivy?" he asked.

"She's with Clark." Eden clipped Lily into her seat.

"Clark?" Archer started the truck, frowning. Who the hell was Clark?

She glanced at him, suddenly nervous. "My ex-husband arrived. He volunteered. Ivy was sleeping, so I figured he could handle it."

The son of a bitch was here. Talk about exercising self-control. He glanced at her, hearing more than she said. "Not too hands-on?" He pulled the truck onto the highway and headed toward the ranch.

She shook her head. "He loves them, but they're not a...priority. If that makes sense. I'm not sure it does."

"You're amicable?" he asked. He couldn't imagine how that worked. But then, he couldn't imagine letting Eden go.

"We try. He's not really a bad guy. Just not family material." She paused, stroking Lily's brow. "He wanted...more."

He watched the sweep of her finger, the way Lily's brow relaxed, and smiled. More? Than his wife? His daughters? "Sounds like his priorities are out of whack," he mumbled, taking her hand in his.

They settled into a comfortable silence. It was easier to breathe now, knowing his father was in good hands. And having Eden with him. Everything was better with her.

She squeezed his hand. "Your father is going to be okay, isn't he?"

"The CT scan tomorrow will tell us more. But hopefully, it'll be a matter of resting." He turned his hand over, threading his fingers with hers. "I think we're all willing to take turns making sure that happens."

"Clara, too," she added.

"You're okay with that?" he asked, curious.

"She deserves happiness. I think your father makes her happy." She ran her thumb across the back of his hand. "What about you? Are you okay with the two of them?"

"It's good." Never in a million years had he imagined his father letting another woman into his heart. But Archer had never been in love or shared a connection. Losing that, being alone, would be hard. If his father had found someone to love, who loved him, he had no business interfering.

"You're a good son, Archer Boone." He liked hearing her say that. And felt no small amount of pride at her words.

He parked the truck and carried Lily's car seat inside.

"See, she's home." A man was holding Ivy. Ivy, who was crying. "She's home."

"Momma, where did you go?" Ivy wailed, tears streaming down her red-cheeked face. "I can't find Mr. Snuggles. And you were g-gone."

Archer frowned.

Eden crossed the room. "I'm so sorry, Ivy. You were asleep and Daddy wanted to stay with you. Mr. Teddy had a big fall and I went with Archer to see him in the hospital."

Ivy was still sniffing, her breath coming in little puffs of air. "I-is h-he okay?" she asked.

"He's gonna be fine, Ivy, don't you worry," Archer said.

Ivy nodded, still sniffing. "I couldn't find you," she said, burying her face in her mother's neck.

Eden sat, holding Ivy close. "Did the storm wake you?"

"Uh-huh," Ivy said, relaxing against Eden.

"I'll put Lily to bed," Archer said, heading into the suite. He sat Lily's car seat on the dresser and unbuckled the clip, lifting her little body close. She stretched before curling into herself with a sigh. He smiled, placed her into the crib and covered her with one of the blankets.

He stared down at the baby, hoping Lily would stay asleep for her mother. Ivy's tears had subsided, but the sharp tones of Eden's and Clark's voices let him know things were far from peaceful. As much as he'd like to pull Eden into his arms and have a long night's sleep, he knew that couldn't happen. He wasn't raised that way. Before he took Eden Caraway back to his bed, she'd know what he wanted. And it wasn't sex. Well, not just sex. He loved her. Now he just had to find the courage to tell her. And if need be, beg her to stay.

Chapter 13

It was hard to ignore Clark pacing in front of the windows that lined the back of the Lodge. His expression was tense, his movements agitated. And while Ivy was already drifting into an easy sleep, Clark kept glancing her way. He was truly upset.

"It's not your fault, Clark," she offered, touched that Ivy's tantrum had affected him so. "She's a bear when she's woken up."

"What?" He paused, looking at her. "Oh. I... I'm so out of practice."

She couldn't argue with him about that. But he was the one who broke their plans, not her.

"His father going to be okay?" Clark asked.

She nodded. "Hopefully."

He sat opposite her, leaning forward to rest his elbows on his knees. "What are you doing, Eden? Do you know how upset your dad is?"

"I'm tired of living my life around his moods, Clark. Contrary to popular belief, I have marketable skills. I can get a job somewhere else."

"In Texas?" Clark shook his head. "Your dad's got a pretty long reach." He paused. "But I'm not just talking about you here, Eden. I work for him, too."

She stopped rocking Ivy. "He won't fire you, Clark. He loves you. He made that perfectly clear during the divorce."

Clark stood, pacing again. "What about the Boones? You think they'll find donations rolling in if your dad's blacklisted them?"

She stood. "So the plan was to come here and back me into a corner? Make sure I knew that rebelling would lead to dire consequences for everyone?"

Clark shifted on his feet, his hands on his hips. "You think I like being in this situation? We might be divorced but, for crying out loud, I still care about you. I love Ivy and Lily. If I had another solution, I'd share it."

She stared at him, a sinking feeling in her stomach. "What does he have on you?"

Clark's expression shifted, as if her words insulted him deeply.

"Knock it off, Clark. Tell me the truth," she whispered, fearful of waking Ivy.

He deflated. "I never could get anything past you."

She waited.

"I might have been caught taking Mrs. Bryant to a hotel room after the Spirit of Giving Ball," he mumbled, avoiding her eyes.

"Mrs. Bryant as in the wife of the chairman of the board?" She shook her head. "And…"

"You come back with me or we both lose our jobs and I will undoubtedly get blacklisted, if not my ass kicked." Clark shrugged.

She shook her head. "Your inability to keep your penis in your pants stopped being my problem the day our divorce was final."

Clark had the decency to look chagrined. "Eden, I'm asking for your help."

"No, you're not. Asking for help would be helping you find a new job. Someplace far away." She kissed Ivy's head.

"Eden—"

"Clark, go to bed. It's been a long day, and

honestly, I need time to think," she murmured, breathing Ivy's scent deep.

Clark hesitated, his gaze bouncing between her and Ivy.

"What?" she asked.

He opened his mouth, then closed it. "Nothing. I'll see you in the morning. Ivy was telling me there's a big Labor Day parade?"

She stared at him. "I'm not feeling very celebratory at the moment."

"So he's staying?" Clark asked, pointing at her bedroom.

Right. Archer was in her bedroom with Lily. Chances are he'd heard their entire horrible conversation. The perfect way to end her evening.

"You barely know the guy—"

"Are you kidding me?" She headed toward her bedroom. But there was a ring of truth to Clark's words. She'd known Archer only a week. A week and he was putting her children to bed and treating them like they were his own. That wasn't normal, was it? She should have her guard up, be cautious. Instead of aching for his touch and the comfort of his arms.

"Come on, Eden, you'd freak if I did *this*," he chided.

"Did what? He's taking care of Lily so I can deal with Ivy. You should be thankful he was here or you'd have to actually engage with your children."

Archer chose that moment to stroll out of her room. His expression was neutral—guarded. "She's sleeping," he said, acting like he hadn't intentionally walked in on their fight. "Guess I'll turn in."

She knew there was no way he could stay, but she'd hoped they'd have time to hold each other. After Clark's verbal minefield, the thought was doubly appealing. But Archer's day had been long and stressful. In his gorgeous blue eyes, she saw the tension. She crossed to him. "I know tonight's been… stressful."

He stared down at her, making it easy to pretend there was no one else in the room. "Dad was lucky. We all are." His gaze fell to Ivy, sound asleep in Eden's arms. "She needed her momma."

Eden nodded, smiling. "Nice to be needed. But I should put her to bed."

His jaw locked, a slight crease forming between his brows before his gaze shifted to Clark. "I'm staying in Dad's room here if you need anything. Get some sleep."

She nodded, wanting to hug him, to burrow closer. "You, too."

He ran a hand over Ivy's head, hesitating only briefly before cupping her cheek. "Night, Eden."

She smiled up at him. "Night." She shifted Ivy and headed to her room, shutting the door behind her. She tucked Ivy in, stroking her soft curls and planting a kiss on her silky cheek. She didn't know what the hell she was going to do, but she'd find a way to make it right.

Somehow.

For all of them.

She tossed her clothes aside, the simple act of brushing her teeth wearing her out. She took a quick shower, smoothed on some moisturizer and headed to bed. But Clark's coat and briefcase were there. And the box of her mother's letters was sitting on the floor by the nightstand. Not stored underneath the bed, where she'd left it earlier.

"Clark Caraway," he said, offering Archer his hand.

"Archer Boone." Archer shook his hand, trying not to smile at the intentional pressure the man used. If the man needed to feel strong, he could squeeze Archer's hand all he wanted. Archer knew the truth. Clark wasn't strong. Hell, as far as Archer was concerned, Clark wasn't much of a man.

"I appreciate you helping Eden with the girls," Clark said.

Archer waited.

"She's got a lot on her plate. Always going," Clark continued.

That much was true. But he still wasn't sure what this man was looking for. As far as Archer could tell, Clark Caraway was one of those men who used his looks and charm to make things easy. His brother Ryder could have been like that, but he'd been too hotheaded for anything to be easy. But that wasn't the only difference between Ryder and Clark. Ryder would never try to put his problems onto someone else. No one should. No man should.

"She's an amazing woman and mother," Archer said. Not daring to add, "and you're a stupid son of a bitch for letting her go"— even though he was really tempted.

Clark's smile dimmed, the tic of his jaw muscle revealing he wasn't all smiles, after all. "She is. But she's not as tough as she acts. She's lonely, that's obvious. And one of the reasons her father sent me after her."

Archer bit his tongue. He had no idea where this was going, but he was more than a little curious.

"She's been pretty sheltered her whole life. Her parents, even me. Something about Eden makes you want to protect her." He paused.

"Protect her from what?"

"Opportunists. She's one of two heirs to a huge fortune." He sighed.

Which was news to him. "You're not giving her much credit." Archer crossed his arms over his chest. "Eden's too smart for that."

Clark arched a brow, sweeping Archer with a head-to-toe inspection. "Guess we'll see."

Archer was so surprised, he laughed. He'd never considered Eden's monetary situation. If she was set to inherit money, he knew exactly what she'd do. She'd do good things, give generously, not hold on to it or use it for personal advantage.

"She takes work and family very seriously. And even if she fights with him, she's a daddy's girl. What he says, goes," Clark said.

"I'm not the one going through Eden's things or taking things that aren't mine." Archer watched Clark's reaction, wishing he'd had the time to read the letters Clark Caraway had tucked into his briefcase.

Clark's face tightened, his gaze bouncing to the chair and couch.

"You left your coat in her room. And your bag. And the letters." Archer stepped closer. "Guess Ivy waking up threw a wrench in things."

Clark shook his head, staring up at the ceiling. "It'll hurt her."

"Is that what this is about?" he asked. "Protecting her?"

Clark glared at him, the muscle in his jaw working. "I don't know what you think you know about me—"

"I just met you," Archer interrupted. "Everything I know about you, I'm learning right now."

Clark's smile was hard, his chuckle forced. "Did you put the letters back?" he asked.

Archer nodded.

"You have no idea what you're doing." Clark stared at him, his anger rolling off of him.

"The only thing I'm doing right now is going to bed," he said. He didn't know what was in the letters or why Clark was so upset, but he'd done what he thought was right. He hoped it was the right call.

Clark brushed past Archer. "I'm doing a site review on Tuesday before I take Eden and the girls home."

Archer didn't bother to turn around or say a word. Only after he'd heard Clark walk up the stairs and down the hall and close his room door did Archer allow himself to relax.

He was tired, but there was no way he'd be getting any sleep tonight.

His mind was spinning. His father. Eden. Her father. Clark. No point lying in bed when his brain wouldn't shut off.

That was the good thing about the refuge—always something to do. He'd check on River. Toben said he'd taken care of him, but he knew the horse would be distraught. A lot of them didn't like storms. Like Fester. He could only hope the fences had held and all the animals were where they were supposed to be.

"Archer?" Eden whispered. "Is Clark still here? He left these." She held out Clark's coat and briefcase.

He shoved his hands in his pockets and shook his head. Seeing her, hair loose, long white nightie, bare toes, was all too tempting. He knew just how soft she'd feel pressed up against him.

She smiled. "You always do that."

"What?" he asked.

"Put your hands in your pockets," she said. "When you want to reach for me."

He swallowed. "Is that so?"

She nodded, dumping Clark's coat and briefcase on the floor and crossing the room to him. She stood inches away, staring up at him. But something out the window caught her eye.

"Fireflies," he said.

"I haven't seen them since I was little," she said, staring out the window. "I used to catch them with my mom. It was hard work."

"Keep them as pets?" he asked.

She shook her head, frowning up at him. "No, we'd catch them. Then let them go. Didn't want to hurt them."

He stared, studying her.

"You look like you've got a lot on your mind, Dr. Boone."

He nodded.

She reached up, smoothing his brow. "I'm a problem solver. A doer. If you want help?"

He shook his head.

"No? Then I need a favor. It won't take long," she said, her gaze traveling over his face.

"Okay," he agreed, his hands itching to touch her.

She hooked her finger through his belt loop and tugged him toward her door, smiling. "This way."

He followed, ready and willing for whatever she had in mind.

She closed the door behind him, then pushed him forward, toward the bed. "Sit," she said.

He sat.

She lifted his foot, eyeing his boots. "Off."

He smiled, tugging his boots off.

She hopped on the bed beside him. Once his boots were off, she pushed him back on the pillows.

"Eden—"

"Hush," she whispered, snuggling tightly against his side. "I need this, please."

His arms wrapped around her, tugging her close against his side. He closed his eyes, soaking up her scent, the slight weight of her arm and hand on his chest, the silk of her hair as he ran his fingers through the long locks. He felt the moment she drifted off to sleep, the way she went pliant and her breath grew slow and steady. He waited, wanting to hold her all night, but knowing he had no right.

When she rolled over, he slipped from the bed. He tugged on his boots, taking a long look at the woman he loved before he headed to the refuge.

Chapter 14

Eden bounced Lily, wincing as her daughter's shrieks grew louder and louder. She glanced at Clark. "Maybe you should take Ivy," she suggested.

But Ivy's eyes filled up with tears. "Momma, you have to see the parade. Hush, Lily."

Eden took Ivy's hand in hers. "Your daddy can take you."

"Come on, Ivy, we'll have fun," Clark offered. "I can put you up on my shoulders so you can see the horses better."

Ivy frowned, Clark's offer making her rethink her tantrum. "But…but…"

"We'll be right here," Eden said, pointing

at the park. "I bet if I stand on the bench, I'll
see the parade. But Lily won't hurt everyone's
ears with her crying." She tried to tease.

"Stop fussing, Lily," Ivy said. "Please."

Lily sniffed, her feet kicking, then burst
into tears.

"That's not nice, Lily," Ivy scolded. "Momma
likes horses, too."

"It's okay," Eden said. "After the parade,
we'll go see Dr. Archer's horses, okay?"

Ivy nodded. "Okay, Momma."

"Ready?" Clark asked, taking Ivy's hand.

"Yep," Ivy said, skipping. "Hurry."

Eden sat on the bench and put Lily in her
lap. "What's up, little bug?" she asked, kissing the baby's forehead. "Those gums bothering you?" She offered her the teething ring
she'd packed in the ice chest. It was cold,
soothing, and Lily started gnawing it with
a vengeance.

"Better?" Eden asked.

She sat back, watching the crowds gather
on the sidewalk. It was going to be a scorcher.
She didn't miss being packed shoulder to
shoulder in this heat. The sounds of sirens
started, making Lily jump. "It's parade time,"
Eden said, grinning down at her daughter.

Lily returned to gumming her teething ring while Eden watched the people of Stonewall Crossing. Nice people. People who said hello and waved. Like the Boones. Sure, they were curious—she was an outsider. But she didn't feel like an intruder.

Yes, the town was small. But did she need shopping malls or a movie megaplex, massive gyms or supersized grocery stores? Not at all. She needed a home. A place to start over as Eden, not a Monroe. A place she'd want her girls to grow up.

Stonewall Crossing had a lot to offer her.

"Eden." Renata waved. "You're missing the parade." She wore a full getup. Pink plaid shirt, chaps, jeans, boots and a hat with a long feather.

Eden smiled. "I was afraid Lily would deafen the crowd. She's teething. Why aren't you riding?"

"We're bringing up the rear," she said. "I'm late. Just left Dad."

"How is he?"

"Good. Growling like a bear to get out." She paused. "Wanna walk with me?" Renata asked. "Since she's calm?"

"Sure." Eden shifted the diaper bag and

snapped Lily into the front pack, holding the teething ring close so Lily would stay happy.

"Still planning on leaving soon?" Renata said, leading her through the crowded sidewalk.

"I don't know," she answered honestly. "I was just thinking about that."

"You realize you're his first…girlfriend. Ever. He took our mom's death really hard and I think, and you know I'll tell you what I'm thinking, he doesn't want to go through that again—loss, I mean. So he's made a point of avoiding people and relationships… and feeling his whole life. Until you and your girls." Renata kept walking, but Eden had come to a stop.

How was that possible? Besides the fact that he was brilliant and well-respected, he was smoking hot. Women would notice him.

"Coming?" Renata called back.

Eden hurried to catch up, still processing Renata's words as they rounded another corner and cut through an alley. She watched a fire truck going down the main street, followed by a large tractor pulling a trailer, but Renata's words still echoed.

When Eden finally spied the Boone Ranch

Refuge truck, she was surprised to see Ivy and Clark.

"Who is that?" Renata asked, an appreciative purr to her voice.

"That's Clark, the girls' father."

"Oh." And just like that the tone changed, interest gone.

Eden liked Renata. "What are you two doing here?" Eden asked, grinning at Ivy.

"Dr. Archer said I could ride with him," Ivy said, hopping up and down in pure excitement.

She glanced at Clark. "You're okay with that?"

Clark shrugged. "I want her happy."

"Well, I think it's safe to say you've accomplished that." Her daughter nodded.

He tickled Lily's feet. "Feeling better, Lily-pad?"

"Clark, this is Renata Boone." She saw Clark's eyes widen. He liked what he saw. A lot. He should—Renata was a gorgeous woman. Who deserved way better.

Renata nodded, pulling herself into the saddle.

"Momma said yes," Ivy called out.

Eden turned to see Archer striding toward them. If someone had told her she'd be weak-kneed over a cowboy, she'd have laughed. But seeing Archer, starched, hugged in denim and leather, his tan cowboy hat casting a shadow over his face, made her insides melt.

"Morning," she said, unable to stop her smile.

"Morning," he said, smiling right back.

"Lily's not crying," Ivy announced.

"Because your momma knows how to make everything better," Archer said, his eyes never leaving her face.

"Yup," Ivy agreed. "She's pretty, too."

"She is," Archer agreed.

She was blushing and she didn't care.

"Your mother is beautiful, like you," Clark said, picking up Ivy. "Inside and out."

Archer nodded.

"We gonna ride the horse now?" Ivy asked.

"Yes, ma'am." Archer climbed up and turned, reaching for Ivy. "Remember what I said?"

"Gentle? Whispers?" Ivy nodded, holding her arms out.

"Right." Archer sat her on River, his arms anchoring her in place. "Think you can wave at all the people?"

"I think so," Ivy said.

"We'll be waving," Eden said.

Archer touched the brim of his hat, shooting her a lethal smile, before guiding River toward the street with the rest of the riders.

"The sister single?" Clark asked.

"She has four brothers, Clark. All of whom would have no problem kicking your ass," Eden said with a laugh, astounded at his cluelessness. She headed back toward the road, excited to see Ivy and Archer in the parade.

Ivy was good as gold. She smiled, giggled, held on to his arm and waved at the crowd with all her might. She probably had half of Stonewall Crossing won over; he knew he was. She chattered away, asking the name of everything and what it was for. And since Archer appreciated an inquisitive brain, he answered her.

By the time the parade was over, her questions had faded and she'd shifted, leaning into him with her head against his stomach.

"Look at you, all sweet and fatherly, holding a sleeping beauty," Renata said. "Pretty little thing. Like her mom."

Archer didn't disagree.

"Speaking of her mother." Renata nudged Blue closer. "You realize you're running out of time."

"And you realize I've known her for a week?" he bit back.

"You don't love her?" Renata asked. "And her kids?"

"I do," he answered, surprising both of them into silence.

Renata stared at him, her blue eyes round.

"Knock it off," he muttered.

She shook her head. "I'm in shock."

"Stop it." He sighed.

"I can't." She grinned. "You know what you need to do, right?"

He waited, shooting her a cautious look.

"You need to take her on a date, just the two of you. Lay it all out there, tell her how you feel."

"She can't just leave Lily and Ivy in a stall for the evening," he argued.

"I can watch them. And if Dad knows what's going on, I'm sure he'll let Clara out of his room for a few hours." Renata smiled. "Since she got here, you seem…happy."

He was happy.

"You don't want to lose that."

No, he didn't. Her leaving scared the shit out of him. If she left, she might not come back. What the hell would he do then? But just because he was acting irrationally didn't mean she was. "I think it might take more than one date to convince her they belong here with me."

Renata smiled. "Well, you won't know until you talk to her."

He couldn't argue with that. But talking to her scared him almost as much as her leaving. He didn't say much as they rode to the trailers and trucks waiting to haul the horses back to the ranch. No Eden, so he turned River and headed out onto the streets.

He stopped now and then, letting tourists and kids alike pet River's neck. The horse stood, tolerating the affection until Archer set off again.

He saw Eden amid the crowd, Lily sleeping in the sling, shielding her eyes as she looked for him. She waved when she saw him, her smile bright and sweet.

He urged River on, riding down the middle of the road. "I think I have something of yours," he said, glancing at Ivy.

Eden laughed. "She's worn out. You made today unforgettable, Archer."

He smiled. "I hope so. Looks like Lily's down for the count, too?"

"Nap time," Eden agreed. "Clark went to cool the van down."

He nodded, then cleared his throat. "You free for dinner tonight? Renata said she'd watch the girls. I was hoping I could have you to myself."

"The girls are a handful—you know that."

"She has nephews. Lots of nephews. I think she can handle your girls," he said.

Eden nodded. "Okay."

Damn if he didn't want to smile like an idiot. Instead he asked, "Where are you parked?"

"The lot by the creek," she said, pointing.

He nodded, keeping River at a slow walk.

"Why is it called Weeping Woman Creek?" she asked. "Kind of sad."

"It's a sad story," he said.

"Tell me. I love history, learning about a place's origin."

"Settlers would stop here for water. Some thought to stay, set up camp along the creek, close to water. They were working on houses, tiny cabins, but it was a start. They were still sleeping in their wagons when a flash flood hit. The men and women tried to save the horses and livestock. But the water rose and the current swept the wagons away. None of the children made it."

Eden stared up at him. "That's really really horrible, Archer."

He nodded. "I think it was meant as a warning to those passing by. Creek still gets dangerous when it rains. Banks are too steep." He saw the look on her face, her grief. "I'm sorry, Eden. I should have made something up."

She smiled up at him. "No, you couldn't. It's nice to know I'm always going to hear the truth from you. Even if it's sad." She chewed on her bottom lip then, her eyes shifting from him—almost nervous.

He smiled. The truth. He may not be outright lying, but he wasn't telling her something. Something big. Something she needed to know. And tonight, when it was just them, he'd find a way to tell her he loved her.

Clark appeared and said, "Need an escort?"

Archer scooped Ivy up, savoring her slight weight in his arms before delivering her safely to Clark. The man might be their father, but Archer didn't like him. He couldn't.

"Thanks again," Eden said, resting her hand on his thigh.

His hand covered hers as he looked down at her. "I'll see you around six?"

"Yes." She sighed, pulling her hand from his and loading Lily into the van.

He rode back to the truck, loaded River

into the trailer and took Renata's truck to the hospital.

He was dusty and dirty, but he needed his father's advice.

"You look like you've got a storm cloud following you around," his father said as he stepped inside the hospital room.

"I guess I do." He looked at Clara, then sat in the chair at his father's bedside. "How are you?"

"Fine," Teddy said. "Itching to get home."

Archer glanced at Clara.

"Tomorrow morning," she said.

"That's good. So nothing on the CT?"

"A thick skull." Clara patted his father's shoulder.

"Didn't need a CT scan to tell me that." Archer grinned. "You'll survive one more night."

"You're not the one getting poked and prodded, a damn light shining in my eyes every two hours," his father grumbled.

Archer chuckled.

"What's eating you?" his father asked.

"I'll go get some coffee," Clara offered.

"No, stay." Archer sighed. "It's about Eden."

Clara sat on the bed by his father.

"Go on," his father prodded.

"Give me a sec," he said, running a hand over his face. "I'm taking her out tonight—Renata's watching the girls… Thing is, I love her. I want her and the girls to stay."

"Say that," Teddy said.

Clara smiled. "Teddy—"

"I can't just throw it out there," Archer argued. "She deserves more."

Clara shook her head. "Archer, hearing that will be enough, I promise you. Love has always come with strings and addendums for Eden. Always. If you give her your heart, unconditionally, you will have given her something she's never had before."

He shook his head. "You don't understand, Clara, I'm not an easy man—"

"But you are the man she wants, Archer. This, I know," Clara finished. "Teddy, I am going to help Renata this evening."

Teddy nodded. "I know, I know." He looked at Archer. "When you ask for her hand, you let her know she's getting a family out of this. It might help." He winked at Archer.

"Thanks, Dad." Archer sat back in his chair, pleased to see color in his father's cheeks. And the smile on his face, on Clara's face, was nice, too. He should stay a while, take some notes. He could use some tips on courting a woman, since tonight he was going to propose to the only woman he could see a future with.

Chapter 15

Eden soaked in the tub, reviewing the proposal she'd finished for the refuge. She knew what the board looked for and could find no objective reason to deny funding. Especially since she now had proof that her mother wanted to support the refuge. She hadn't had to read through the last packet of letters; her mother had stated clearly that she wanted to use her inheritance for a charitable endowment for the refuge after her first visit.

She'd scanned the letter and added it to the proposal. That alone should warrant the board's approval.

But she'd learned so much more about

her mother. How disillusioned she was with life. How unhappy and unloved she'd felt. How alone she was. Her parents had whole-heartedly supported her marriage to her father—wealth married wealth. Two powerful, ambitious families combining. Even if her mother was lost in the shuffle.

Coming to the refuge, she'd felt free of all the restraints and expectations her life placed upon her. Eden related to that.

She toweled off and slipped into the only dress she'd packed. Soft blue cotton with tiny white flowers and a ribbon under her breasts. It was feminine and pretty, exactly how she wanted Archer to see her tonight. She tied on her sandals and brushed through her hair, leaving it down. He liked running his fingers through her hair. She liked it, too.

And if dressing to please him would ease what she had to tell him, she'd do it. Her stomach was in knots, anxious for the night to begin—so she could finally get the weight of this horrible lie off her chest. If he could forgive her, love her, was another matter al-together.

"Momma, you look so pretty." Ivy smiled. "Beautiful."

"Thank you." Eden kissed the tip of Ivy's

nose, breathing deep to calm her nerves. "No tears tonight?"

Ivy nodded. "No tears. But Lily might cry. A lot."

Eden smiled. "She might."

"No promises," Ivy continued, shrugging.

"Maybe you can help Renata?" Eden suggested.

"I'm a good helper," Ivy agreed.

Eden took her hand and let Ivy lead her from the bedroom. Lily was on a blanket, furiously rocking on her hands and knees.

"One day soon she's going to take off and we're all going to be in trouble," Clara said. "You look so nice."

"Yes, you do." Clark was not pleased.

Eden had decided the best course of action was to ignore him.

"I really appreciate you coming," Eden said to Clara. "I know you'd rather be at the hospital."

"Eden, you are my family. These are my girls, too. Teddy understands. I will see him in the morning." She patted her cheek. "It's good, you taking time for yourself."

Eden glanced at the clock, surprisingly nervous.

"He won't be late," Clara said softly, her eyes sparkling.

"I brought cupcakes. And a horsey coloring book. And a movie with horses," Renata said as she came in.

"Ooh." Ivy ran to her. "I love horses."

"I thought so. We still need to get you some boots, Ivy. But we'll start with this." She pulled a pink straw cowboy hat from the large bag she carried and plopped it on Ivy's head. "Let's see."

Ivy tipped the hat back, smiling broadly at Renata and Clara before turning toward Eden. Eden grinned, dropping to her knees. "Don't you look precious," she said, adjusting the hat just right. "I like it."

Ivy played with the string beneath her chin. "You need one so we can match. And Lily, too."

Lily cooed, making Eden look down. At Lily, right by her knee. "Lily?" Eden's voice was thin. "Did you crawl?"

"She did," Clara said, clapping her hands.

"First thing I saw when I walked in the room. Lily going for her momma," Archer said, a huge smile on his face.

Eden blew out a deep breath and scooted

back, holding out her hands. "Show me, little bug, come on."

Lily wobbled, rocking back and forth, before crawling rapidly across the floor and into her mother's lap. Lily's giggle had the whole house laughing. Eden scooped her up and hugged her. "You're growing up, little bug," she said, pressing kisses all over her face.

"She's gonna be a big bug?" Ivy asked.

Eden laughed. "Soon." She hugged the girls close. "But not too soon."

"You two have fun," Renata said. "We girls are going to have a great time."

Eden stood, holding Lily close. "She'll wear herself out, that's for sure. No wonder you were fussing earlier. You knew something big was coming, didn't you?"

"I'd say going mobile's pretty big," Archer agreed. "Speedy little thing, too."

Lily smiled at Archer, reaching for him with splayed fingers.

"Yes, she's adorable." Clara took her. "And she will be just as adorable tomorrow."

"So go on," Renata agreed. "Ivy, tell Mommy and Archer to go so we can color horses."

"Bye, Momma!" Ivy waved wildly.

"Fine. Have a good time," Eden said, looking up at the man who stood inches from her. "You ready?" she asked, her nerves returning big-time. She couldn't lose him.

He nodded, his slight smile warming her through and easing her nerves.

She followed him out the front door, waiting as he closed it. But she wasn't expecting him to tug her around the corner. Or press her against the wall, one hand on either side of her head. She held her breath, loving the look on his face as he bent slowly to kiss her.

"I've been waiting to do this all day," he whispered.

She leaned into him, gripping his shirt with both hands. Her lips parted beneath his, wanting more. Hearing him groan, feeling the slide of his tongue against hers, made her hold tighten. Her arms slid up, wrapping around his neck for balance.

He broke away, pressing a kiss to her nose. "Let's go."

He took her hand in his, but stopped at the top of the stairs. She peered around him, absolutely mortified to find his brothers and cousins standing on the bottom step—in various stages of shock and amusement.

"Archer," Hunter, the oldest, called out in greeting.

Ryder started to say something, but Hunter elbowed him hard in the gut.

Archer sighed, shooting her an apologetic look before leading her down the stairs to his waiting truck. He held the door open for her, acting like they didn't have an audience, even though her cheeks burned with embarrassment.

She could only imagine what they said after Archer pushed her door closed. Whatever it was, they were smart enough to keep their voices down. But even then, she saw the slow shake of Archer's head and his reluctant smile.

By the time he'd climbed into the truck she was giggling.

He took one look at her and laughed, too. "Guess I should apologize for them, but…"

She shook her head, still laughing.

He started the truck and backed up, waving a hand at the group still watching their every move.

"You look good in blue," she said, meaning it. His eyes were as clear as the Texas sky.

"Same," he said, shifting gears and taking her hand. "You're beautiful, Eden."

She smiled. "I feel that way when I'm with you."

His gaze locked with hers, so intense and heavy she found breathing difficult. He swallowed, turning his attention to the well-rutted dirt-and-gravel road. They bounced along, the view growing more pastoral—they weren't headed to town. It took a few minutes before she realized where they were going. But once she did, she relaxed. There was such an energy between them, being in public was hard. Going to his place would give them the privacy to talk through the laundry list of things they needed to talk about.

After they were done diffusing the charge of want and hunger that filled the truck cab.

Archer's nerves were on high alert. He'd planned out what would happen. He'd escort her to his house, feed her dinner, talk to her and go from there. Losing his head was not part of the plan. But he hadn't counted on how damn beautiful she was. How sweet her smile was. Or the way her laugh ignited a hunger deep inside him. It'd been a struggle to wait until they were on the porch. But once they were there, he'd had to touch her. And taste her.

It hadn't been enough.

His brothers would never let him forget it.

Not that he cared. They'd all made total jack-asses out of themselves when they'd found their wives. Guess it was part of the court-ing process.

But now that they were here, parking in front of his place, all the things he'd wanted to tell her sounded too harsh or too flowery. He climbed out of the truck and came around, but she met him halfway, taking his hand in hers.

"How's your dad?" she asked, the scent of her perfume tickling his nostrils as he opened the front door.

"He's good. He'll be home tomorrow morn-ing." He pushed the door shut behind them, tossing his keys on the table.

"How's River?" she asked.

He smiled. She would think about his horse—and it made him happy. "I think he's okay. He was a little shy of me at first."

"Poor thing. I'm sure he knows what hap-pened." She ran her hand along the back of the couch. "Do you think he feels guilty?"

He nodded. "Absolutely."

"So how do you tell a horse it's not his fault?" she asked, sincere.

He stepped forward, cupping her face in his hands. "You talk to them, wait for them to come to you, then give them physical and verbal comfort. They know. They're far more intuitive than humans. A touch, a look, spacial proximity. The connection with them has to be genuine—something they feel."

"Is this close enough?" Her gaze met his as she slid her arms around his waist. "Touch?" He felt her fingers grasp his shirt, pulling it free from the waist of his jeans, before she pressed her hands against the skin of his back. He shuddered from the contact. "And look?" Her voice was husky. She was just as affected as he was. Her eyes were warm, inviting. But it was more than desire. He felt it.

He shook his head. "No doubt about the connection."

"No?" Her breath wavered.

"No." His mouth brushed hers, his heart thumping like crazy. "Hell, no." He wrapped one arm around her waist, his hand stroking her soft hair.

Her hands wound along his back, her fingertips tracing his spine. He arched into her, pressing the soft curves of her breasts against his chest. His groan was caught in her mouth. Her lips clung to him, soft, yielding. Her offer was too sweet to refuse. Wanting her, the ache surging in his blood, was all that mattered.

Her hands gripped his shirt before splaying wide to stop him. "Wait, Archer," she gasped.

"I don't want to," he argued, nuzzling the side of her neck.

Her breath hitched when his lips latched onto her earlobe. "I know… Me neither… but…" She pushed again, putting the slightest space between them. "It's important."

He waited, his eyes searching hers. "Then tell me."

She nodded, clearing her throat. "Hold on." Her hands still gripped his shirt, making it impossible to miss her agitation.

"You're shaking, Eden. Talk to me." He anchored his arms around her waist, keeping her close.

She nodded. "I… When I arrived at the refuge I'd had a bad day."

He nodded, remembering their first encounter all too clearly. "And I ripped into you."

"You thought I was someone else." She shook her head. "And I went along with it… Because I didn't want to be who I am. I thought it would be easier. It gave me an in, a way to be there without being the…enemy, I guess. I'd do my job, compile my reports for the board and leave. You, your family, would never know the truth."

Archer stared at her, her words making no sense. "The temp job?"

"No. I'm not a temp… I just let you think I was." Her voice wobbled. "For too long."

Archer's nerves went cold, his stomach leaden. "What job?"

"Let me explain, please, first." She spoke softly. "You need to understand."

He frowned. "What job?"

"I'm a grant administrator for Southwest National Bank. And one of the foundations I manage is the Monroe Foundation." She swallowed. "I'm Eden M-Monroe. Caraway was my married name."

His hands slid off her shoulders, but he never looked away. Monroe. "Why lie about that? I don't understand." He could tell there was more coming; her face said it all. He stepped back, forcing her to let go of his shirt, and crossed his arms over his chest.

"You said you'd never felt trapped. But I am." She shook her head. "People I don't know treat me differently because of that name. It's the thing that keeps me chained where I am—that puts up an obstacle for every door it opens. My life is about negotiating, sacrificing, fighting to be heard." She broke off. "Being here…being someone else, freed me for a few days."

He turned slowly, staring down at her. "I need a minute."

"I came here to prove myself to my father. To show him I was worthy of the family name, that I was worthy of his respect. But now I know I don't want it. His name or his respect. All I want is—"

"How were you going to do that, Eden?" Archer asked, his throat tight. "No more lies."

She swallowed, wrapping her arms about her waist. All the color faded from her cheeks. "He wanted to deny the refuge more money—"

"Why?" Archer snapped.

She paused.

"What was his reason?"

"Things weren't being accurately reported. Money was being…misused."

"So you came out here to prove it? You came to help him?" His heart seemed to stop.

"Archer, I know it sounds bad—"

"Lying about who you were helped with that," he cut her off. "I'd have been less obliging to hand over my finances to you in the state they were in. Not to hide anything."

"I know." She stepped forward. "The refuge—"

"Why keep lying then, Eden?" Her name stuck in his throat. "Looking for other ways to gain your dad's favor? Humiliating me, maybe? Making me think…" He broke off. No way he was going to admit what he'd planned tonight. He was a damn fool, so caught up in soft skin and big, guileless eyes that he never thought what he was feeling wasn't real. Wasn't true. "Did you find anything?" His voice rose slightly, anger kicking in. "Is your daddy going to be proud?"

"You know I didn't," she said softly. "Archer, if I could go back, I would. I hate myself for lying. I should never have let things get so far. Never. This is all wrong."

He couldn't breathe. He wasn't sure what was worse: that she'd lied or that she would go back and change things. Her words gutted him, cutting his heart loose and leaving him to bleed out.

"You need to leave…" He stared at the ceiling, searching for something to ease the roar in his ears. He hurt, a ripping, crushing pain that he hated. "I don't need your money, Eden Monroe." He glanced at her. "I don't want it. All I want is for you to go." He crossed the room, grabbed his keys and offered them to her. "Go."

"Archer, please listen to me." Her voice wavered.

"No point now. Hard to take much stock in a liar's word." He opened the door, ushering her out. "Tonight was goodbye, anyway."

She stood still, staring at him. "I don't... I'm not a liar."

"Really?" He shook his head, his temper threatening his control. "Eden. Go." The words were razor sharp, slicing through him, jolting her into movement. "I'm asking nicely. Just go."

She walked to the door, taking the keys from him. Her fingers brushed his, stirring all the things he needed to forget. He jerked away from her, shoving his hands into his pockets.

"Leave the keys at the front desk," he said, avoiding her gaze. "Tell the girls..." He broke off, hating the burn in his eyes and the fresh pain that sliced through him. It wasn't just Eden he'd loved. And lost. "I'm sure you'll think of something to tell them."

She hesitated on the porch, but he shut the door. Once the truck started, the sound of crunching gravel faded, he rested his forehead against the thick wood surface. It didn't matter that he ached to go after her, to hold her, to love her. What he wanted was a lie. She was a lie. What had he expected? A person didn't fall in love over a matter of days.

Love was an illusion. He'd just let himself forget that fact for a while.

Chapter 16

Eden sat in the truck cab until she was cried out. Her head throbbed and her heart felt like it had been kicked around, but that would fade in time. No one had ever died from a broken heart. Besides, Eden had two amazing reasons to keep going. Right now, she hoped they were both having sweet dreams so she could finish off a bottle of wine and sleep until sunrise. And tomorrow, she and the girls would fly back to Houston so Eden could go over her findings with the board.

Whether or not Archer still wanted her support, he—the refuge—had it.

She slid from the truck and climbed the stairs, going around to the back of the Lodge.

Clark sat in one of the large wooden chairs, reading papers.

"The girls asleep?" she asked.

Clark jumped, dropping the paper and standing. "You scared me."

"I got that," she said, stooping to collect the paper he'd dropped. But the paper wasn't what she expected. "Why are you reading my mother's letters, Clark?"

"You okay, Eden?" He frowned. "You look a little shaken up."

She glanced at the letter in her hands, the words blurring as the evening's events flashed through her mind. Considering how much she'd cried, her eyes were probably bloodshot and her makeup was a wreck. She blinked, wiping fresh tears from her eyes and staring at the letter she held. Her mother's handwriting.

How many notes had she tucked into Eden's lunch box? Or phone messages had she taken, clipping them to the front of the refrigerator door. She used large, feminine loops and flowing lines... Eden skimmed over the letter. One she hadn't read...

She stopped, blinking again.

She read the line again.

And again.

Her mother had cheated on her father. No, that wasn't right. Her mother had cheated on her husband. On Jason Monroe. With a man named Dylan Quaid. A horse wrangler here on the ranch. Eden was the result.

She sat in Clark's chair, reading the two lines that forever changed her world over and over again.

"Eden?" Clark's voice was soft.

"Is this why you're here?" she asked, not bothering to look at him. She didn't need his answer. His briefcase sat on the ground by the box of letters. Two letters lay inside his briefcase. She stooped, placing the letters on her lap. "What were you planning to do with them?"

Clark didn't say anything.

She stared up at him then. "Damn it, Clark, you owe me an explanation. What the hell is going on? Just the facts, nothing else. And I mean nothing."

Clark sighed. "Your mom told your dad about this when he wouldn't give her the divorce. Guess she hoped he'd give her the divorce if he knew the truth. Greg told me. He listened to the whole damn argument."

"So everyone knows but me?" she asked, cradling the letters against her chest.

"No. Only Greg, your father and me. If your dad had it his way, no one else would ever know." Clark shrugged.

"Why?" She lay back against the chair. "I'm sure he's relieved I'm not his."

"Her will. It specifically says her money is to be given to the father of Eden Jane Monroe, and the father of Gregory Ryan Monroe. Meaning he'd have to give half to your...dad." Clark knelt beside her. "I'm sorry."

Eden stared at him. Then past him.

The stars stretched out overhead, the only constant currently in Eden's life. That, and she was alone. "What's in this for you?"

"He didn't want you to find out. Thought maybe you'd find something here to reveal the truth."

"If I hadn't found you tonight I would never have known." She shook her head. "That's terrifying. I would have kept trying and trying to win his love... Kept trying to figure out what was wrong with me. And you'd have let me." She stooped, riffling through Clark's briefcase.

"That's all of them. Eden?"

"No more." She stood, waving him away.

She clutched the box of letters tight and pushed through the back door. Music was playing softly, the smell of popcorn scenting the air. Renata and Clara were talking, animated. But to Eden, everything seemed to be moving in slow motion.

Renata and Clara stopped cleaning and froze, their expressions growing more alarmed with each passing second.

"Eden?" Renata asked.

"What happened?" Clara asked. "You're so pale. Sit."

Eden sat, still holding the box. She stared into the empty fireplace, imagining how cheery it would be during the winter months. She could imagine this place then, wrapped in lights and full of smiling faces.

"Drink this." Renata pressed a glass into her hand.

Eden took a sip, wincing at the sting of whiskey. "Whoa." She blinked, eyeing the glass. It burned all the way down to her belly, knocking the haze away and waking her up. "Thanks."

Renata nodded. "You okay?"

She shook her head. "Not yet."

"You told him?" Clara asked. "What did he say?"

Eden glanced at Renata, embarrassed and ashamed.

"Oh, dad told me. I admit I was surprised, but I figured Archer would get over it when you told him you loved him." Renata frowned. "Guess it didn't go well?"

"I didn't get the chance to tell him I loved him," she said, taking another sip of the whiskey. "He told me to leave. He w-was furious." She felt the tears building and sniffed fiercely. "He told me to leave his refuge, that he didn't want me or my money."

Renata sat beside her, hugging her close. "That sounds like Archer. He's downright mean when he's mad."

Eden didn't think he was mean. He was right.

"I'm sorry, Eden." Clara took her hand.

"Oh, it gets better." Eden sat up, wiping the tears away and pulling her mother's letter from the box. She handed it to Clara and sat back, watching both the women's faces as they read the latest revelation.

"Holy shit," Renata said. "I... What are you going to do?"

Eden rested her head on the back of the couch and closed her eyes. "First, I'm going to present the board my findings and get Archer his money. Second, I need to find a new job. And a place to live. And—" she paused, taking Clara's hand in hers "—a new nanny."

"I'll go with you, Eden. Of course I will," Clara argued.

"I won't let you, Clara. It's time for me to stand on my own two feet. Besides, Teddy needs you. And you, I think, need him. I'm not going to be responsible for you missing out on something this good." Eden hugged Clara tightly and smiled up at Renata, refusing to let either of them know just how close she was to falling apart.

Archer walked behind his father, watching his every move. They'd argued over the use of a wheelchair and a walker, but Teddy Boone had insisted on walking into his own home. And while Archer worried over his father, he respected his need to be independent. The fall had shaken them all in different ways.

"Look at you," Renata said, pressing a kiss to his cheek as soon as they walked through the doors.

"I'm walking." His father sighed. "I've been walking since I was a year old. I hardly see it as some sort of accomplishment now."

Renata rolled her eyes. "Glad you're home, Dad."

"Glad to be home. Why is it so quiet?" he asked.

"It'll be loud enough in an hour. The whole family's coming over," Renata said, pressing a kiss to his temple. "Want some iced tea?"

"Sounds good." He nodded, staring around the great room of the Lodge. "Good day?"

Archer glanced in the direction of the suite, the tug almost unbearable. "Yep."

"How's the little paint horse?" his father asked.

"Fine," he mumbled, tearing his eyes from the door.

His father saw him. "Where are Clara, Eden and the girls?"

Renata came in, glass of iced tea in hand. "Clara drove them to the airport this morning, Dad. She was stopping at the grocery store before she came home. Something about making you a German chocolate cake?"

They were gone? Archer tried not to react to this announcement. It was his own damn fault. He'd told her to leave. And she had.

His father turned, frowning at Archer. "And you didn't think to mention this?"

Archer put his hands on his hips. "Didn't know."

His father's eyebrows rose. "What happened?"

"Nothing," Archer said.

"Really?" His father stared at him. "Sometimes I don't know what to do with you, boy. You want to end up on your own? You like sleeping alone?"

"No, sir." Archer tried to keep his tone neutral. Tried and failed.

His father's brows went higher. "Why'd you let her go?"

"I didn't let her go. I told her to go." He ran a hand over his face.

"She had a lot to sort out, Dad," Renata interrupted. "Who knows, she might be back. She's looking for a job now. I know that much."

"She is, is she?" his father asked.

Archer stared at his sister. "What are you not telling me?"

Renata shook her head. "You wouldn't listen to her, but you're willing to listen to me?"

Archer blew out a deep breath, staring at the hardwood planks beneath his feet. "She lied—"

"She lied, but she regretted it. Did you give her a chance to explain?" his father yelled.

Archer remembered her words all too well. She regretted more than lying. "She wasn't here to help the refuge."

"Not in the beginning," his father agreed. "In the beginning, she came here to win her daddy's love. In the end, she wanted yours."

Archer stared at his father. "Doesn't matter now." He didn't want to think about Eden right now. His father was home; his family was coming together. That would keep him preoccupied—for now.

"You remember Dylan Quaid, Dad?" Renata asked.

Archer did. The man had been his personal hero, teaching Archer all about horses. He'd had a gift few men had—the ability to calm a horse, to understand them, befriend them. For five years he'd followed the man around, watching, asking questions, taking notes. When Quaid disappeared in the middle of the night, Archer had missed the man's quiet ways. "What about him?"

"He's Eden's father," Renata said, her blue gaze fixed on him.

"What?" he asked, stunned.

"Her mom's letters?" his father asked.

Renata nodded. "Funny thing is, I think she was relieved."

Archer paced the great room, then stopped. "She okay?"

Renata smiled.

"Is she?" he repeated, trying to imagine how she was feeling. Alone. No, damn it, she wasn't alone. He ran a hand over his face, pacing the floor. She had him—if she wanted him. He didn't know what she wanted or how she felt; he'd cut her off before she'd had a chance to clear that up. About damn time he found out.

"She's strong," Renata said. "Hard to tell."

Because she knew how to keep it together. She'd had years of practice. The time had come for her to let someone else take care of her. To let someone who loved her help shoulder her burdens and lighten her load. Archer glanced at the suite door, then back at his father. "Dad, I gotta go."

Teddy nodded. "Bring her home, Archer."

Archer nodded, all but running from the Lodge to his truck. He spent forty minutes trying to get a flight to Houston. But no matter how they tried, the layovers would mean he'd arrive sometime late tomorrow. And he didn't want to wait.

It took three hours to get to Houston, putting him there around ten. Late, but hopefully not too late.

He spent the time flipping radio stations, anything to keep his nerves at bay. He'd been stupid to get too stuck in his head. She'd asked him to listen, but he wouldn't. If he had, what would she have said?

And her father? Had she been alone when she'd learned the truth?

He punched the steering wheel.

"Stubborn son of a bitch," he ground out.

By the time the Houston skyline and latticework of highways sprang up, Archer's patience was slipping. Every car and truck, motorcycle and minivan, seemed intent on slowing him down. He cussed, his boot hovering over the brake as he wove among traffic.

She lived in a neighborhood of small homes on a neat and tidy street. Each house looked the same, manicured bushes and a tiny yard. Not enough room for the girls to play in. He felt pinned in the farther down the road he went.

A moving truck was parked in front of Eden's house.

He climbed out of his white Boone Ranch Refuge truck and stared at the front door. It was now or never. He walked down the concrete walkway and knocked on the door. But he doubted she'd hear his knock over Lily's crying. Poor little bug needed to cut those teeth.

He rang the doorbell and stepped back, the light by the door coming on and temporarily blinding him. He heard the squeak of the front door as it opened.

"Archer?" He'd managed to surprise her. "Wh-what are you doing here?"

He stared at her, taking in her tousled hair and smudged eyes. "Can I come in?"

She blinked, clearly confused. "Okay." She stepped back, bouncing Lily on her hip.

He knew she was watching him, wondering what the hell he was doing there. But he wasn't ready to talk—not yet. He needed to ground himself or he'd screw things up. He stared around the small house. It was in chaos. Packing paper, Bubble Wrap and boxes covered the floor and most of the furniture.

"Moving?" he asked. "All this in, what, a few hours?"

"I'm being evicted." She smiled. "Jason Monroe doesn't like being made a fool of. Or being proved wrong."

Archer waited. "This isn't about the refuge, Eden. Tell me it isn't."

She shook her head. "It's not. It's about the truth. Doing what's right. Renata told you? About…about my mom and my…dad?"

He nodded.

"After I gave the board members a copy of my report on the refuge, I reminded them my mother was an advocate and she wanted to help the refuge whenever she could. Jason wasn't happy…but the facts speak for themselves. Once that was done, I quit. I wished him well, told him I was going to find my father and that if he tried to stop me from finding work, from fending for myself, he'd regret it."

She's never looked more beautiful to Archer. Strong and defiant. He was proud of her. And sad for her. No matter how hard she tried to hide it, he knew she was hurting. Hell, he was hurting for her.

She shifted Lily, patting her little back. "It's okay, little bug."

Lily sniffed, her breath hiccuping as she rubbed her eyes.

"Past your bedtime, little bug," he said, his voice low and soothing.

Lily looked at him, yawned and reached for him.

"Can I?" he asked.

"Archer." Eden's voice broke. "Why are you here?"

He took Lily, cradling her close and patting her back. "I came to get you."

She frowned, shaking her head.

He cleared his throat, trying not to get lost in how beautiful she was. And how much he wanted to touch her. "Come home, Eden."

She backed away, wrapping her arms around her waist. But then she stopped, her spine stiffening as she faced him. She looked just like she did that first day, all cold indifference. "So this is some sort of rescue mission? To save me? Did it ever occur to you that I don't need to be rescued?"

He swallowed again, clearing his throat. "You don't. I do."

And just like that she melted. "Archer—"

"I love you. I need you and the girls. You're my family." He broke off. "I'm hoping you can forgive me for…being an ass."

She was blinking rapidly. "And my lie, can you—"

"Forgiven." He shook his head. "I don't want us moving forward with secrets or regrets."

She stepped forward then, pressing her hand to his cheek. "I only regret that it wasn't me you were in love with. Me, me. Not Eden Caraway."

"You're you, Eden. You're the woman I love with my whole heart. And if you'll have me, if you'll let me, I'll be the best damn husband and father I can be."

Her hazel eyes bore into his, searching. "At the ranch? In Stonewall Crossing?"

He nodded. "It's a good home. Good enough for you, for Ivy and Lily. If you want." He knew she could say no. After his outburst, he wouldn't blame her. But he hoped. Oh, how he hoped.

"I do? Yes," she agreed. "The best home." She smiled.

He could breathe, finally. "Then marry me." He cupped her cheek, knowing his hand was shaking and there wasn't a thing he could do about. "You know I love you, that I need you and the girls. You know I'm stubborn and…uptight at times. But I'm asking, anyway. Eden, will you marry me?" His voice was gruff, thick.

"Yes, Archer, yes. There's nothing I want more." She stepped closer. "I love you. I'll always love you."

He lifted her left hand, sliding a thick metal band onto her finger. "It's a ring I made from a horseshoe nail. Wish I'd bought you something pretty, but I didn't think—"

"It's beautiful. More so because you made it." She stared down at the silver nail he'd shaped and polished. The ring he should have given her the night before. She rested her hand on his chest and looked at him. "I never thought I'd see you here. In the city—away from the ranch and home."

He grinned. "You are home, Eden. Though I'm not a big-city driver." He loved her giggle, the way she melted into him when he pulled her close. "Whatever you want, whatever you need, I'll do my best to see you have it." He brushed his lips against hers.

"I already do. My girls are happy. I'm happy." She pressed a kiss to Lily's cheek, smiling at the sleeping baby, before standing on tiptoes to kiss his lips. "I have you, Archer Boone."

Epilogue

Archer carried Lily past the first stall, admiring how closely she paid attention to everything he did. She was going to be like her mother, a horsewoman through and through.

"Hee," she said.

"Horse," he agreed.

She smiled at him.

He walked on, glancing again at Eden in the pasture. She was standing next to her father, Dylan Quaid. The two were in deep conversation over Fester and his blind lady love—the little paint now named Kitty. Ivy stood between them, her pink cowboy hat and brown boots—with sparkles—shining in the mid-morning sun. Dylan had arrived a few days before their wedding. And in the three weeks since, he and Eden had grown closer every day. It warmed Archer's heart to see her finally get the love of her father.

Not that accepting her mother's infidelity was easy. It wasn't. Archer had held her many a night, wishing there was something he could do or say to make the hurt she felt ease. Eden knew that her mother must have really loved Dylan. And the last pack of letters had proven that.

Holding her seemed to help both of them. He held her a lot. He went out of his way to let her know he was, and always would be, there—loving her. But lucky for him, she did the same. A smile here, a touch there, a kiss on his cheek when he sat at his desk. He was a happy man.

"Hee," Lily repeated as River stuck his head out. "Rivi."

"Yep, River's saying hello." Archer stood close enough that River could explore Lily with his nose. She was like her momma, keeping her hands down and staying still. Respectful of the animal.

"He likes you, Lily," Archer said, smiling

as Lily stared into River's eyes. "You're his little bug, too."

She smiled at Archer, four little white teeth showing. "Rivi."

"Any plans this morning?" Eden asked, walking into the barn with Quaid. "Clara and Teddy wanted to take the girls into town to get food for the kitten and a new jingle ball."

"Taffy will love that." Archer chuckled. Ivy had her orange tabby. Taffy ran all over, especially in the early morning hours. Her favorite thing to do, other than playing with Ivy, was batting her jingly ball down the staircase. "Can we look into a ball without a bell?" he asked.

"Tired?" Eden asked, sliding her arms around his waist and dropping a kiss on Lily's head. "Part of fatherhood, Dr. Boone. Sleepless nights."

"I'm not complaining, Mrs. Boone," he assured her. "But the bell seems like asking for trouble." He kissed her temple, drawing in her scent. "If the girls are going into town, I can think of a few things I'd like to do with my wife."

Eden's cheeks flushed, her gaze falling to his lips and making him ache to be back in their bed.

"Hey, hey, now," Dylan said. "Let me take Lily up to the Lodge so you can kiss her proper, boy. A man's got to do what a man's got to do—and that means keeping his wife happy."

"Yes, sir." Archer laughed, letting the older man take Lily.

The family resemblance was incredible: same winning smile and same astounding ability with horses. Eden was a wonder. Her father seemed intent on passing on his knowledge, and she was just as intent to master it. Now Fester wasn't the only horse that got excited to see her. The animals responded to her presence. And it was a joy to watch.

"See you soon, little bug," Eden said. "Thanks, Dad."

"Ma-ma-ma," Lily chanted. She turned her big eyes on Archer. "Da-da."

"Don't you fret, Lily-pad. Momma and Daddy will be back soon. They just need some time to love each other. Mommas and daddies do that," Dylan said as he carried her toward the barn doors. "You're a lucky little bug, growing up surrounded by so much love."

Archer agreed 100 percent.

"She's not the only one," Eden said. "I have

no doubt I'm the luckiest woman in Stonewall Crossing."

"You are," he agreed, loving the way she pressed herself against him. "You got me."

She laughed, the sound echoing in the barn and warming his heart through.

* * * * *

Get 4 FREE REWARDS!

We'll send you 2 FREE Books plus 2 FREE Mystery Gifts.

FREE Value Over **$20**

Both the **Romance** and **Suspense** collections feature compelling novels written by many of today's bestselling authors.

Get 4 FREE REWARDS!

We'll send you 2 FREE Books <u>plus</u> 2 FREE Mystery Gifts.

FREE Value Over **$20**

Both the **Harlequin Intrigue**® and **Harlequin**® **Romantic Suspense** series feature compelling novels filled with heart-racing action-packed romance that will keep you on the edge of your seat.